KEEPING SECRETS FROM THE BILLIONAIRE

A BAD BOY, ALPHA MALE, BILLIONAIRE ROMANCE

LEXI AURORA

✽ Created with Vellum

FREE BOOK

Want to meet another hot, alpha, Billionaire? Join my readers group, Lexi's Sexies, today and get an exclusive story.

http://eepurl.com/cR9bWT

Join Lexi's Sexies Today!

KEEPING SECRETS FROM THE BILLIONAIRE

JULIE

I've had my taste of ritz and glamour, and it did nothing but bite me in the ass. Now I'm living as best I can and taking care of my son. I'd go to hell and back to protect him. So when richer-than-God Graham Porter walked into my life, I swore to myself that I wouldn't let him seduce me. I had too much on the line, and I knew just how it would end.

But God...his kisses are addicting, and his fingers know just where to touch me. Maybe I could indulge just once or twice. I just need to remember that at the end of the day, he was my boss, and he'd never fall in love with someone like me.

GRAHAM

I've been burned by love before, and I know better than to get involved with my sexy-as-hell personal assistant. She's got a kid, and I know she's looking for that happily ever after. What women isn't? But I can't resist that perfect body and that sensuous mouth.

1

JULIE

The red neon light for the motel was going bad. It buzzed and blinked all night long, turning my dingy two-bedroom room into a disco party. Tyler had danced himself into exhaustion, but then, that kid could sleep through anything. It was a blessing that he'd been a quiet baby, or I probably would have fallen apart. While I couldn't even begin to imagine my life without him, the circumstances of his birth hadn't exactly been the highlight of my life.

When morning came, I dragged my exhausted, sweaty self out of bed and into the shower. The water was as cold as the air was hot, but even the lack of hot water and air conditioning wasn't enough for me to try to find somewhere else to live. With my budget, the fact that the place was relatively bug-free and came with a mini-kitchen was more than I could ask for.

"Baby, are you up?" I called out as I brushed my wet, strawberry-blonde hair into a ponytail. With a four-year-old son to chase after and very little money, I didn't bother with make-up. It'd simply melt off anyway. I'd made my way to

California thinking I could raise my son in warm and sunny climates, but Las Pameros was mostly desert, and the sun baked everything in its path.

"Momma, did you get some blueberry Pop-Tarts? I think I'd like some blueberry Pop-Tarts." My ever-so polite son rubbed his eyes as he walked into the bathroom and stared at me. With his blue eyes and blond hair, he was almost the spitting image of his father.

Pretending to think it over, I narrowed my eyes and studied him. "If I remember correctly, I told you yesterday that I would only get some blueberry Pop-Tarts if you could recite the information that I gave you."

"My name is Tyler Garner Dennings. My mother's name is Juliette Christie Dennings. I am four years old." He went on to correctly announce his address and the new phone number that I'd given him to memorize since I'd lost my phone three days ago and had to get a new one. My stomach twisted as he correctly recited the number for the local police and went over the stranger danger rules. In a year, he would be five, and I'd have a decision to make. It wasn't fair to keep moving him around when he started school, but it was also dangerous to stay in one place as well.

My kid was smart, and I wasn't just being a biased mother. He picked up things quickly, and he absorbed everything around him. It was almost a little terrifying.

Stumbling over a few of the numbers, he righted himself and looked at me with hopeful eyes. "Well," I declared loudly. "I think that might get you two blueberry Pop-Tarts!"

"Two!" His eyes shined with excitement, and I nodded my head as he skipped from my bathroom into the kitchen. It was a good thing that he was already ready because I was running late.

Pulling on a pair of jean shorts and a button-up plaid

top, I slipped my sunglasses on my face and grabbed my things. My only friend and pretty much savior, Crystal, lived two doors down. Crystal didn't have any kids, but she worked out of her motel room and was more than happy to keep an eye on Tyler for me while I was at work. There was some sort of unspoken rule around here about not asking people why they'd ended up at the Sunny Side Up Motel, so I never asked Crystal her story, and she never asked me mine, but I'd felt obliged to give her some details. She did look after my son, and there was always the slightest chance that his father might turn up.

Crystal was about my age, twenty-seven, with the perfect body and a gorgeous face. I couldn't help but sigh with a little jealousy when she opened the door and her perfect rack bounced ever so slightly when she bent to give Tyler a hug. While I had those childbearing hips and an ass that I still claimed carried some baby-weight, my tits were pretty small.

Not like there was a damn thing I could do about it.

"Are you giving me half of your blueberry tart?" Crystal gasped as she accepted the gift. "Well, that's so sweet. You must know that I have something special planned for lunch."

"What's that?' Tyler asked while I whipped out my phone and connected with Crystal's Wi-Fi. The motel internet was a joke, and Crystal had her own separate connection that she let me use.

"If I tell you, it won't be a surprise!" Crystal looked up expectantly. "Long day ahead of you?"

I knew that she thought my job was weird, and the truth was that I knew it was a little strange myself. I needed a cash-under-the-table kind of job, and I found it when I'd answered an ad for someone to run errands. By errands, my boss basically wanted to pay me a sliver of what she made to do her job. Darleen Mason was the personal assistant for the sinfully wealthy and handsome Graham Porter, but it was obvious that Darleen wasn't as interested in the work as she was the man. So while Mr. Porter paid her to keep his personal life organized, I was the one actually doing the work.

The truth was that it was a helluva lot better than some of the other jobs I'd done in the past, and Darleen never missed a payment.

"It looks like Darleen's boss has a birthday coming up." I'd signed a non-disclosure agreement, so I wasn't allowed to say who I was working for, but Crystal knew that it was some bigwig. "I have to pick up a present for him."

Crystal pursed her lips in disapproval. "I keep telling you, Julie. Something doesn't smell right about this job. How do you know you're not working for some mobster or drug kingpin?"

"You should be a writer," I laughed. "I'm fairly certain that isn't the case because things like that don't happen to me. Tyler, baby, I've got to run. Come give me some sugar." As always, when I left him, my emotions ran a little high, and my old Texas twang showed its ugly head. I'd worked hard to keep that accent down, but it popped up far more often than I would have liked.

My perfect son ran into my arms and gave me a big kiss on my cheek. I held him tight and inhaled deeply into his hair. He was the reason that I still breathed, and the reason that I was even doing all of this.

"Crystal says she's got something special for lunch," he whispered in my ear. "Last time she did that, we got McDonalds!"

God help me when things like McDonalds thrilled my

son. I let him go and paid Crystal for the day. The damn sign for the motel was still buzzing and blinking as I started my piece-of-crap car and drove to the boutique shops on Quarter and Main.

When I first started working for her, Darleen had given me a credit card to authorize expenses. I worried that someone would ask to see some identification, but it would seem that all the employers on the strip knew Darleen by heart and were told that I wielded her card. I hated using it. While Darleen had given me a job and paid me on a regular basis, that woman had a mean streak a mile wide. She threatened hell on earth if I ever used the card for personal reasons or if I ever told her boss what was really happening. When we did meet, the woman did nothing by criticize me up and down, but I tried not to mind. After all, I wasn't doing this for me.

I was doing it for Tyler.

Stepping into Matheson and Sons, the curio shop, my eyes immediately landed on a gorgeous wooden model ship that was encased in glass. The raw beauty of the ship spoke of someone's love and expert craftsmanship. It was unique, and it'd make a perfect ship for Mr. Porter. Generations ago, his family had made billions off the shipping industry, and while they had their hands in different pies now, I knew from my research that Graham Porter had a thing for ships.

"My nephew carved that," a gravelly voice said with pride. "His father would rather him be a lawyer, but it's rare to see that kind of talent these days. If you're interested, we can personalize the ship with a name of your choice."

"Your nephew has a gift," I said with a small smile. There was a time when I loved to be out on the water in a sailboat or kayak, but those days were long gone. "I'm actually here to pick up something that you're holding for Darleen Mason?"

The hope vanished from the man's face, and I immediately felt bad. The ship was out of place in a shop like this, and I gathered the man was having a hard time selling it. Moving slowly, the owner rounded the desk and reached under to pull out a box. When I opened it an peered inside, I immediately grimaced.

Nestled inside was the most god-awful looking statue I had ever seen. It was two lovers wrapped around each other and dipped in gold paint. If she gave that to Graham Porter, she might lose her job, and then I'd lose mine.

At least, that's what I tried to tell myself when I made the order to have Porter Shipping personalized on the carved model ship and returned the statue. The truth was that Darleen would never know until it was too late, and then she'd never admit that the ship wasn't her idea when she saw how happy it made her boss.

Maybe she'd even give me a raise.

I finished the errands and rearranging Mr. Porter's schedule, and the gift was ready just before the store closed. I paid for the gift-wrap and headed home. Maybe tonight, the damn sign would be out completely, and I'd be able to get some sleep.

2

GRAHAM

I stared in frustration at the computer in front of me and tried not to smash it to bits. There were a million things on my to-do list, and I couldn't remember the first one of them because my personal assistant had called in sick and failed to email me my schedule like she normally did.

Miles, my cousin, lounged in the chair across from my desk and kicked up his feet. We looked similar enough with dark hair and green eyes that he could have been my brother, but as far as personality went, we were night and day. I was reminded of that as I eyed his polished sized-thirteen shoe on my clean desk. "Don't you have something else to do other than bug me?" I snapped. "I thought you were leaving for New York today."

He chuckled. "Who knew that the great Graham Porter would be defeated by a computer calendar? Why don't you just call the damn woman and ask her to email it to you? Surely a cold wouldn't keep her from that."

"I tried," I muttered darkly. "I'm fairly certain that she's getting lipo or more Botox done. She was pretty much yelling at herself while she stared in the mirror yesterday."

My cousin shuddered. "Is there anything natural about that woman?"

Everything about Darleen Mason, from her permed, bottle-blonde hair to her bejeweled toenails were fake. I still wasn't sure why the hell she worked for me because I wasn't paying her nearly enough for those Double-Ds or the calf implants that she'd gotten to make her legs look shapelier. "Her eyelashes fell off the other day," I grunted. "Why the hell do women wear fake eyelashes?"

"She's hoping a few more surgeries might finally make her pretty enough to land you as a husband," Miles barked with laughter. "If only she knew how much you hated gold-diggers."

It was part of the reason that I would never settle down. Women were fun, hell, women were a necessity, but they were only good for a night or two before they started dreaming about glittering diamonds and shiny new cars, and hell would freeze over before I trusted a woman enough to deck her out in jewels.

"I've got it," I said with relief when I finally found the link to the calendar. I was about to click it when a notification for an email popped up on her computer.

Calendar Changes and Birthday Present.

"Fuck," I hissed. "I think Darleen is getting me a birthday present."

Miles' feet hit the ground, and he sat up in the chair. "Is it naked pictures? I'm dying to see if those things look as fake as they feel."

Lifting an eyebrow, I stared at my cousin. "And when exactly did you feel up my personal assistant?"

"When she *accidentally* fell into my lap the other day,"

Miles said with a frown. "I almost let her fall to avoid touching her, but I guess I'm not as big of an asshole as I'd like to be."

"Good. Maybe she'll start planning on marrying you instead of me," I said absently as I opened the email. It was addressed to Darleen from some woman named Julie, and it just confirmed that my present had been retrieved, and she'd made the changes to the calendar. *Suddenly sick my ass.* Darleen had clearly been making arrangements to have the next few days off.

When I closed the email, I realized that there was a long thread of messages between them.

Six-months long.

Scrolling through, I felt a wave of fury. "You've got to be fucking kidding me. That stupid, lazy bitch."

"Whoa. What the hell is wrong with you?"

"Darleen has been paying someone to do her fucking work for six months. For six months, someone named Julie has been given private information about my life." My eyes widened. "My God, Darleen gave her the notes from the investors meeting to type up."

"You thinking its someone working on the other side or someone from the press?" Miles asked tightly. A plane accident from five years ago left Miles and me as the only two remaining Porters left, and he had as much interest in our money as I did.

"I don't know, but I'm about to find out." Tension built in my shoulders as I composed an email from Darleen to Julie requesting that she meet me at the house so we could discuss some private details about what I wanted her to do next.

When she emailed me back and said that she wasn't comfortable meeting me at the house, I knew that I had her.

"She must be someone that we know. I'm going to kill Darleen. I'm going to sue her for breach of contract, and then I'm going to make sure that no one who makes over twenty-thousand a year will want to fuck her."

I shot off another email insisting that I had private financial papers that needed drafting, and I couldn't have her do it in public. She emailed me back almost immediately agreeing.

The trap was set, and I was eager to see who I was about to catch.

"I guess I'm going to need another assistant," I growled as I slammed the laptop closed. The fake rhinestones glued to the top sparkled in the sunlight, and I had an urge to throw it out the window.

"Maybe make sure this one isn't going to pay someone else to do the job for them," Miles laughed.

"You think this is funny?" I demanded. "We've got millions tied up in this online banking company. If this Julie person really is a corporate spy, we could lose all that money."

"That would suck," Miles agreed. "But it's just a few million. I think we'll still get by. Have you made a decision about tonight?"

"You mean am I going to go out with you so you can have a shot with the triplets?" I asked as I stood and stretched. I was about to turn him down; the truth was that it had been too long since I'd had someone in my bed, their lips locked around my cock. This whole situation with Darleen had me desperate to blow off some steam.

Still, there was work that needed to be done. Regretfully, I shook my head. I needed to make sure my head was clear when I met this Julie person tomorrow, and I didn't need another woman in my bed aiming for holy matrimony.

3

______

JULIE

Meeting Darlene at the mansion broke her number one rule, but I couldn't tell the woman no twice. She was already likely to be a little pissed when she realized that I'd changed out his birthday present.

With the gift and Graham Porter's dry cleaning in my back seat, I drove my squealing coupe up to the intimating rod-iron gates and pushed the button. They'd probably never seen a car like mine. The damn thing was three different colors, but then I'd spent less than a grand on it.

I got what I paid for.

"Are you lost?"

Snorting at the indignant voice on the other end, I rolled my eyes. "No, sir. My name is Julie Dennings. I'm here to see Darleen Mason."

To my surprise, the interrogation went no further, and the gates opened with a loud creak. I eased my foot off the brakes and my car protested loudly but rolled through the mighty entrance.

I didn't have much experience with wealthy homes. Graham Porter was absurdly wealthy whereas Jonathan

Bright and his family had only been moderately wealthy. Their multi-million-dollar home was the pride of small-town Connecticut, but here in Los Pameros, you could spit a watermelon seed and hit a billionaire. Why all the wealthy flocked to the desert was beyond me.

The long drive was covered in lush cypress trees, and the rest of the grounds were just as meticulously kept. When I passed a small lake with a spurting fountain, I nearly laughed. Graham Porter didn't strike me as the fishing type, so God only knows what he'd want with a lake in his back-yard. Maybe he enjoyed spawning west nile virus-ridden mosquitoes.

I parked my car at the entrance of the huge brick home and lugged my things out. My shorts rode up my thigh, and I cursed my bad luck. I really needed to do some clothing shopping if for no other reason than the clothes that had fit me five years ago were now just a little too tight. It wasn't that I was gaining weight. In fact, since I was saving up to get a more permanent apartment for Tyler and me, I hadn't been eating much and was losing weight. The problem was I didn't have time to hang my clothes dry, and the dryer was shrinking them faster than shrinky dink toys.

By the time I'd situated myself and had gathered my things, I had an audience. An elderly man in a suit stared at me disapprovingly. Jonathan had a butler. It seemed like the only way someone rich could prove that they were rich was by hiring an old man to be a butler.

"Ms. Dennings," he said in a low voice. I was almost disappointed that he didn't have a British accent. "If you'll follow me."

I noticed that he didn't offer to help me with my things, but he also looked like he might fall over at any minute. He did, at the very least, hold open the large mahogany doors.

"If you'll wait in the lounge here, someone will be right with you."

"I'm waiting for Ms. Mason," I reminded him helpfully in case he'd forgotten. My arms were straining from the awkward angle I'd been carrying everything, so I practically dropped the clothes on the floor before carefully sitting the gift box on the coffee table. I was still fluffing the bow when I heard the door open.

"Oh God." The words flew out of my mouth, and I flushed. It wasn't Darleen walking towards me with anger in her eyes but Graham Porter himself. My mouth instantly dried as I took my first good look at the man. Pictures didn't do him justice. From the clean-cut square jaw to the grey-tints of his gorgeous green eyes, everything about him screamed power. His thick, dark hair curled at the nape of his neck, and he was built like a wet dream. If his sensuous mouth hadn't been pressed into a hard line, I might have swooned on the spot.

Might have. My swooning days were over.

"Mr. Porter," I said nervously. "There's a very good explanation for this. Have you seen Darleen?" I was going to lose my job, and then how would I get my son out of the Sunny Side Motel? He was a smart kid. Sooner or later he'd start asking why some of our neighbors had different men over every hour.

"I'm afraid that Darlene is out sick," he said softly. God, his voice was smooth as butter. "I didn't expect you to be southern."

"Funny, I didn't think you'd expect me at all," I said as I cleared my throat. "The accent only returns when I'm nervous or angry."

"And what do you have to be angry about?" He walked around me slowly, appraising me.

I was not some horse that needed examining. Enough was enough. I stepped back until I was flush against the couch. At least now he'd have to stop circling me. "Not angry. Just nervous. I was given the impression that I'd never be meeting the boss's boss. You should know that I signed an NDA, so you don't have anything to worry about."

"Darleen signed one of those too. I guess she was hoping to keep you her dirty little secret." His gaze fell to the clothes on the floor. "It looks like you don't do the job much better than she does."

"The gift is fragile," I said hurriedly as I bent to pick them up. "Your clothes are not." I held them out for him to take, but he just stared at me until I carefully laid them on the arm of the couch.

Was the room sealed off? The more Graham Porter stood there and eyed me, the harder it was for me to breathe. The seconds ticked by, and for the life of me, I couldn't think of a damn thing to say. Finally, I thrust the gift box at him. "Look, Mr. Porter, obviously there's something going on here that shouldn't be. I'm not trying to start trouble. I just needed a job, and Darleen provided that for me. I mostly just ran some errands for her. Like this birthday present. She needed a present for you, and I picked one out."

His eyebrows lifted, and I realized my mistake. "Picked it out or picked it up?"

I didn't lie. "Look, the point is that you are obviously not happy about me, so I'll just be on my way." Without my last payment, and damn it, I needed groceries. Tyler couldn't live on Pop-Tarts forever.

"You did more than run errands," he said silkily as he took the box and slid his fingers across the wrapping paper. The tape came off cleanly, and I couldn't help but wonder if

Graham did everything else as neatly as he was unwrapping this box. "You typed up important financial information."

The palms of my hands began to sweat. Just how much trouble was I in? My thoughts darted back to my conversation with Crystal yesterday morning. Maybe I was better off with a mobster or drug kingpin. "It was just a few numbers. I didn't keep any of the information on my computer."

Reaching in, Graham pulled out the ship. For a second, he just stared at it. When he did speak, his voice was rough. "I sure as shit know that Darleen didn't pick this out for me. Why don't you just tell me who you work for, and we can come to some sort of arrangement. I'm a rich man. I'll double your salary."

What the hell was he talking about? "I work for Darleen. She pays me minimum wage."

"Minimum wage?" he choked out. "Ten dollars an hour?"

"No," I said slowly. "I make eight dollars an hour." I knew I should have negotiated more. Now I felt like an idiot.

He lowered the ship and sighed. "I did a background check on you. You haven't been in California long. Before that, you've lived in four different states in four years. Your last permanent address was in Connecticut. You've got no ties with any of the industries here in California, and no ties with the press. Why did you take this job?"

"Darleen seemed like a lovely woman to work for." Okay, maybe I could lie if the situation really warranted it.

He barked with laughter, and, to my relief, didn't ask me any more questions about my past. I'm sure a background search would show that I had a son, but since his father wasn't listed on the birth certificate, and our engagement never reached the press, I had hoped that Jonathan Bright would still be my secret.

"As it is, I'm looking for a new assistant. The only reason that I kept Darleen on was because she seemed so efficient at the job, but it would seem that honor goes to you. I'll pay you salary, and I can promise you that it's a good deal above eight dollars an hour. You already know what the job entails, but you'll be doing it here. My life is very private, and I intend to keep it that way."

His voice was clipped and professional, and I longed to jump at the offer. "Darleen paid me cash," I said in a strangled voice. My cheeks heated at the fact that I even had to ask. "I need to keep that arrangement."

"Why?" he said sharply. "Your background check didn't raise any red flags, but I won't have any illegal work at this house."

"It's not that," I assured him quickly. I gave him the same lie that I gave Darleen. "I owe the government some tax money, and they seized my bank accounts. I need the cash so I can still keep a living wage and pay them off as best I can."

Great. Now that was twice that I had lied to him. Things weren't really off to a great start.

"Fine. You can start tomorrow morning." He seemed almost angry as he walked towards the door, but he stopped and looked back at me. "The present is beautiful. Thank you."

"Darlene's credit card paid for it," I said stupidly, but he had already left the room.

Stupid, stupid, stupid. I had no business agreeing to work for a man like Graham Porter, but all I could think about was that apartment I could get for Tyler. He'd have air conditioning. Some friends to play with. A playground that wouldn't give him tetanus, and walls that didn't shake whenever the hooker next door over-did the fake orgasm.

I just needed to find an owner willing to sublease for cash, but for the right price, that wouldn't be an issue.

The real problem would come when it was time to enroll Tyler in school. Even the threat of Jonathan Bright wouldn't allow me to deny my brilliant son the education that he deserved.

But that was tomorrow's problem, and there was still a pile of today's problems that I needed to handle. I'd cross that bridge when we got there.

4
———

GRAHAM

I've dated women who have graced the cover of Maxim's issue of *Top 100 Hottest Women*. I've fucked A-list celebrities and lingerie models. Hell, I've even seduced a goddamn princess, but not the first one of them affected me as much as the strawberry-blonde woman in old cut-offs and plaid. I could see every freckle on her unpainted face, and I could see about four different tan lines as the shirt fell off her shoulder once again. Her hair was wrapped up in a knot on the top of her head, and her nails were clipped short, but my cock was harder than ever as she bent over the desk to sign the new agreement that I'd set out in front of her.

Ever since I saw that damn model ship, I hadn't been able to keep my eyes off her.

I should have been disgusted. There was nothing I hated more than a woman who couldn't manage her money, and seized bank accounts had gold-digger written all over it, but she wasn't doing anything to get my attention. If I'd seen her on the streets, I'd probably never even look twice at her.

Of course, maybe she was just trying to be the exact opposite of Darleen Mason.

"You're all set," I muttered almost angrily as she signed the last paper. She was now my employee, and I did not mix business with pleasure. I should not have been wondering if her bottom lip tasted as sweet as it looked or if she'd moan or squeal if I sank my fingers in her heated center. "I've already ordered you a new computer. You'll need to transfer the data from Darleen's so I can finally throw that glittery monstrosity into a fire."

"If it makes you feel better, I don't think I've played with glitter since I was twelve," she admitted as she gingerly took the computer. "I wanted to apologize for my outfit. We lost a bunch of luggage in the move, and I haven't been able to replace it, but I promise that I'll have something suitable to wear next week."

I didn't buy that lie for a minute, and I wanted to tell her that the less she wore, the better. *Get a hold of yourself, Graham.* "I never enforced a dress code with Darleen, and I won't with you," I said instead. "She enjoyed wearing dresses to work. The more low-cut the better."

As soon as I saw the look of alarm in her face, I knew that I'd messed up. "All I'm saying is that you should wear what you're comfortable with." I kept my face relaxed as I waited to see what she would do next. Julie bit her lower lip and nodded, and it took all of my self-control not to lean over the desk and taste that bottom lip for myself.

Normally I'd let Daniel, my butler for lack of a better term, give her a tour of the house, but I wanted to stay near her. When I rose and extended my arm, she looked like I might bite her. It was the complete opposite of how most women reacted to me, and it only made me hotter for her. I'd never met a woman that I couldn't have, and part of me, that masculine asshole part of me, wanted to see how long that might last. Not that I wanted to break my no-employees rule with her, but I was confident that I could break through that rough Texas exterior and make her melt.

If I wanted to.

"This will be your office, but you'll have full use of the whole downstairs. There's even a guest room downstairs for if you stay too late one night and need to spend the night."

"That won't happen," she said immediately.

It sounded like a challenge to me, but I let it drop. "Most of the bedrooms are on the second floor, and there's a media center up there. My office is on the third floor, but it's off-limits to everyone. If you need me, you can use the iPads throughout the house to get in touch with me."

"Fancy."

"I can see that you're impressed," I said dryly. "This is just the main house. My cousin spends most of his time in New York, but when he is here, he stays in the East wing of the house. When he is here, I would advise that you steer clear of him. He's incorrigible." And I would have to remind Miles to keep his hands off Julie. He'd take one look at that sexy mouth and decide to have her.

"The West wing is reserved for servants. There are several guesthouses on the grounds as well as a full-sized pool, tennis quarts, a trail through the gardens, and a lake. There is also a fully equipped gym at your disposal."

"Do you even use any of that?" she asked suddenly.

Her question threw me off-guard, and I stopped. "What?"

"You've no wife or children, and it seems like your cousin isn't around much. I'm asking if you get enough use out a full-sized pool and a lake and gardens to make the upkeep worth it? Or is it just for show?"

She was judging me. Even as she looked at me with those big, innocent eyes, I knew that she was judging me because I had money. It wasn't the first time that it had happened. Everywhere I went, there were people who hated me simply because I had money, but for some reason, it bothered me that she would judge me. This woman couldn't get her own financial life straight. She had to be paid in cash so she could survive, and she was going to make me feel bad?

"This house has been in my family for generations," I told her coldly. "And I enjoy every single inch of it."

Julie flushed, and when she spoke, her voice once again had that Texan drawl. "I didn't mean to offend you," she said rapidly. "I just thought that it was a mighty big place for one person."

Fuck, she wasn't judging me. Maybe Ms. Julie really did see something she liked. Hoping to set her straight, I pushed her hard against the wall and tilted her chin up. It happened so fast that she didn't even have time to gasp, and before I knew what I was doing, I dipped my head down and tasted her.

She opened immediately for me, and I swept my tongue over it. Hot. Wet. Inviting. That bottom lip that she nibbled on so insistently tasted every good as I imagined, and before I knew it, I was kissing her like a man possessed. Deep and urgent. It wasn't until I slid my fingers over the bare skin of her thigh that she gasped and pushed me away.

"No!" she hissed.

"No?" I grinned at her. "A minute ago you were telling me that my place was too big for me. I thought you were offering to warm my bed."

"The hell I was," she said hotly. "You can't just push women up against a wall and kiss them like that! You're my boss, and that is inappropriate. I don't want to warm your bed, Mr. Porter. I just want to do a job and get paid. Are we going to have a problem with that?"

Her chest heaved with every breath, and her lips were still swollen from where I'd kissed her. "We won't have a problem as long as you keep your opinions about my life to yourself, Julie."

Walking away from her while I still could, I paused just long enough to look over my shoulder, and I wished to hell that I hadn't. Her fingers were still tracing her lips as though she could still feel me the way that I could still feel her. "I suggest you get started on transferring that data. You have a lot of work ahead of you."

In less than twenty-four hours, she'd nearly made me lose control. Julie Dennings was a dangerous woman to be around, and if I knew what was good for me, I'd stay as far away from her as possible.

5

JULIE

"So he just hired you?"

I leaned back in the chair and popped another greasy potato chip in my mouth. The evening brought some cooler temperatures, so Crystal and I drove Tyler to the nearest park to play. I was hesitant about staying out past dark, but Tyler had been cooped up in the motel for nearly four days straight, and although he never complained, I knew that he needed to get out and run around.

We chased him around for about an hour before collapsing on the bench to watch him play in the sandbox. "Not at first. He thought I was some sort of spy. He even did a background check on me."

Crystal's eyes widened. "Did he find out about your ex?"

"No. I guess he didn't dig far enough. Anyway, he's paying me Darleen's salary and paying in cash, so I'll be able to get an apartment soon."

"That means your name will be on a lease."

I grimaced. "I was hoping to avoid that by subleasing, but Tyler needs to start school next year. I can't afford private tutors to homeschool him, and Lord knows I'm not smart enough to do it myself. I guess eventually I'll have to stop running, but the election will be over by then, and hopefully Jonathan will quit looking for us."

"So what did you say to make Graham think that you weren't a spy?"

I thought about the moment when he'd opened the present and stared at the boat. I knew that was when he'd decided to hire me, but for the life of me, I couldn't figure out what was going on in his head. He was cold and controlled one minute and hot the next. It was enough to give a girl whiplash.

"I don't know, but I think I almost got myself fired this morning. I made a comment about his house being too big, and he kissed me."

"Kissed you?" Crystal gasped.

I shushed her and glanced over at Tyler. I didn't want him to think that there was any trouble between me and the new boss. "It wasn't that kind of kiss. I think he wanted to prove a point."

"That he's a good kisser?"

Just thinking about the kiss made me curl my toes, and I blushed. It had been a long time since a man had put his mouth on me, and I'd never had a kiss like that. "Yes, but that wasn't the point. I think he was trying to prove that he could take whatever he wanted. I think I set him straight."

"From the look on your face, it doesn't look like you set anything straight," Crystal said with a laugh. "It looks like you want him to do it again, and if I were you, I'd let him. You've got too much on your plate, Julie. You need to relax and unwind from time to time."

"I am not going to unwind with the man who pays my bills."

Tyler stood and brushed himself off. For a moment, I

allowed myself the luxury of living in the moment with no worries. He looked so tired that he nearly fell over, but he had the biggest smile on his face. "Momma, I'm hungry."

Crystal started to collect our things, and I ruffled his hair. "Then I suppose I should feed you."

"Can we stop and get some hot dogs on the way home?"

The happy moment was over. I hadn't gotten paid yet, and although I had plenty of food at the house, I only had enough cash left on me to get some gas and pay the motel room for the next week. Quickly, I tried to calculate just how much gas I had in the car.

"I think hot dogs are a great idea. In fact, it'll be my treat," Crystal said with a smile. "I can't remember the last time I had one with all the fixings."

"I'll pay you back," I murmured with a grateful smile. I hated borrowing money, especially when I knew that she wasn't much better off than me, but I also hated to disappoint my son.

"Don't be ridiculous. I would have been inside all night watching television if you hadn't invited me out. Besides, we need to celebrate your new job." She lowered her voice and winked. "And your new man."

I reached over to pinch her, but she was already up and chasing Tyler to the car with a shriek. I'd add some money to the pitiful amount that she charged me to watch Tyler next week. It was strange for me to have a friend, but the more time I spent around Crystal, the more I couldn't imagine my life without her.

The next day I realized that Crystal was right about one thing. Graham Porter had not gotten the message.

I'd worked all morning transferring data from Darleen's computer to my new laptop, and he'd stayed out of my way.

My stomach was grumbling when he appeared in my open doorway.

"Join me for lunch?" he asked in a low voice.

It was a simple lunch invitation between employer and employee, but desire shot through me. How could a man look so tense and so wild at the same time? There was a dark desire in his eyes as he stared at me, but he kept his back stiff and straight as though he were afraid that if he relaxed even for a moment, he'd lose control.

Day two, and I already wanted to fuck my boss on the desk. What the hell was wrong with me?

"I had a big breakfast," I muttered as I kept my gaze trained on the computer. If I looked up, I knew he'd see the lie written all over my face.

"I can hear your stomach from here," he growled and stalked forward. "You're not going to ignore me because of one little kiss, are you?"

"You're not inviting me to lunch because of one little kiss, are you?" I shot back. "Because I have a hard time believing that you ate any of your meals with Darleen."

"You're not Darleen."

"You're right about that," I snapped. "Because she would have welcomed you with open legs, but I am not like that. I just want a professional relationship."

A slow and sexy smile spread across his face. "It's just lunch. We can always make it a working lunch if it makes you feel better."

"Why?" I found it hard to trust his innocent words when his eyes continued to look me up and down like he wanted to eat me for lunch. Lord help me, but my panties were soaked at the thought.

"The last time I ignored my personal assistant and let her do her own thing, she hired someone else behind my back to do her job. Let's just say that I think I should keep a close eye on you."

Was he teasing me, or did he really not trust me? I was just about to agree to a working lunch when my phone rang, and my heart jumped in my throat.

That was Crystal's ringtone.

"Ignore it," he commanded, but I was already scrambling for my purse.

"I can't. It's my babysitter." Blood rushed to my ears as I picked up the phone. "Crystal? What's wrong?"

"Julie, I don't want you to get all upset," she said in a calm voice. "I'm taking Tyler to the hospital, but I wasn't sure if you had insurance."

"Insurance? What the hell does that matter? What happened?"

"He was climbing a tree, and he fell. I don't think he broke anything, but he's got a head wound, and it's bleeding pretty profusely."

"Oh, God." My legs shook, and I reached out to grab something. Suddenly, Graham was behind me with his hand on my back. "Yes, please take him to the hospital. I'm on my way. I'll meet you there."

I hung up and whirled around only to run smack into Graham. "I'm sorry. I've got to go." As I stepped to the side, he moved with me and blocked my path. "What is wrong with you? My son is hurt. I have to go."

"I'm not going to stop you," he said calmly. "But you can't drive in this condition. If you'll give me a second, I'll grab my keys and take you."

"What?" My mind was a jumble, but somewhere in the haze, I knew that I didn't want Graham to meet my son. Still, I was too scared to voice my opinion, and before I knew it, his expensive leather seat was cradling my ass as we flew down the highway.

I would have taken Graham as a man who had someone else drive him around, but he looked comfortable behind the wheel. Even though I had no idea what kind of car we were in, I knew that it was powerful. Graham was the kind of man who craved power.

"I'll drop you off at the emergency door and park," he said as he slowed the car. "I'll come find you. Remember to breathe, Julie."

Breathe. Tyler might fall apart if he saw me in hysterics, so I tried to focus on calming down and counting my breaths as I hurried to the information desk. "My name is Julie Dennings. I'm here to see my son, Tyler. He came in a few minutes ago with a head wound. He's only four years old, and he's my only baby. Please." My voice cracked, and I gripped the edge of the desk.

The heavy-set nurse clicked a few keys on the keyboard and hit a button under the desk. "He's in room 204," she said with a comforting smile as the doors opened. "I believe the doctors are still in there with him."

Gripping the strap of my purse, I hurried down the linoleum hall and tried to block out the sounds. Cries of pain and sobs of grief echoed off the walls. Everything was so white and sterile. I hated the idea of him being here. Too many machines and not enough hugs. By the time I turned the corner into Tyler's room, my whole body was shaking.

"Momma!" Perched on the bed with a pretty, petite nurse wrapping gauze around his head, he gave me a big toothy grin. "The lady is going to make me look like a mummy!"

I nearly melted into the floor. "That sounds like fun, baby. Are you in pain?"

Crystal was pressed against the wall, and her face had gone unnaturally pale. Just looking at her made me terrified all over again, but the nurse just smiled. "Other than the head wound, he seems to be fine. The doctor has already had a look at him, and he isn't showing any signs of a concussion. Head wounds tend to bleed, and they can be terrifying. We've stopped most of the bleeding and given him a couple of stitches."

Tyler grimaced. "That hurt, Momma. Am I going to look like a monster?"

The nurse's soothing voice calmed me, and I reached over to hug my son. As he tipped his head, I could see the patch of hair that they'd shaved and the stitches. Bile rose in my throat when I realized how bad things could have gotten.

"He's a brave boy," the nurse said with a smile. "I'd have some children's Tylenol on hand in case the pain gets to be too much when the excitement wears off. Keep the stitches dry for the next week, and you can take him to his regular doctor to have them taken out. Of course, if you notice any unusual coloring or swelling, you'll need to bring him back immediately."

"Thank you," I murmured as I pressed Tyler to my chest. He squirmed.

"Oh!" The nurse said suddenly. "You must be Tyler's father. I was just explaining everything to your wife. I'm going to print off some paperwork and the discharge papers. If you have any questions, you can ask me then."

For a second, I thought it might be Jonathan standing in the doorway, but it was just Graham. He didn't bother to correct the nurse. "You didn't have to come to all the way back," I said hastily. Why hadn't he just stayed in the waiting room?

"I wanted to make sure that everything was fine." He eyed Tyler coolly, and for a moment, I thought he might bolt.

Tyler was wiggling away from me, and those southern manners that were drilled in me took over. I took a deep breath. "Tyler, Crystal, this is my boss, Mr. Graham Porter. Mr. Porter, this is my neighbor and friend Crystal Smith, and my son, Tyler."

Crystal had a bit more color in her cheeks when she reached out her hand. She murmured a quiet hello, which surprised me. In the whole time that I'd known Crystal, she'd never been shy.

Tyler, on the other hand, wasn't shy at all. "Are you my daddy like the nurse said?" he asked in a serious voice.

My eyes widened in alarm. Tyler had never asked about his father. "No, sweetheart," I said as I stepped between them. "The nurse was mistaken. I was working at Mr. Porter's house, and he drove me here. He just wanted to make sure that you were alright. Okay?" I was desperate for him to understand.

He nodded his head. "Okay. Thank you for bringing Momma," he said politely.

Graham looked completely out of his element as he shuffled his feet. "You're welcome," he said gruffly. "I'll just get a cup of coffee and wait in the waiting room until you're ready."

As he walked out, Crystal let out her breath in one big whoosh. "I hate hospitals. I want to throw up just being here, but he just made the whole trip worthwhile. Jesus, he's even hotter in person."

She had no idea.

6

———

GRAHAM

After meeting Julie's son at the hospital, I spent the next week making sure that I was nowhere near the house when Julie was there. I left a list of things for her to do and then stayed far enough out of temptation's reach. Seeing her with her son was like being dunked in a bucket of ice water. I'd never seen such love in a woman's eyes before, not even with my own mother. I knew right then and there that I could never touch her. Someone like me would only spoil the purity in her.

Unfortunately, there were things that I couldn't avoid, and Darleen's phone call to say that she was coming back to work was one of them. I almost fired her over the phone when I realized what she'd done, but I wanted to see the shock on her face when she realized she'd been caught. I wanted her to know that all of her well-laid plans and dreams for our supposed future were shattered.

I wanted to make sure that Darleen Mason never darkened my door again.

I'd given Julie plenty of work to keep her busy in her

office and told Darleen to meet me on the deck. If I could help it, I wanted to spare Julie from whatever hateful lies Darleen would spout when she realized who had taken her place.

The woman arrived in a skin-tight dress that showed off every curve of her body and was so low-cut that her fake boobs were practically spilling out. She walked confidently on matching stilettos, and when she stepped up to the deck, she removed her designer sunglasses and pursed her pink lips my way. "Did you miss me?" she asked in a husky voice. For a horrifying moment, I thought she was going to try and kiss me.

"Actually, I've gotten along just fine without you," I said coldly and pointed to the chair across from me. "Sit down, Darleen. We have a few things that we need to discuss."

There was real fear in her face, and her eyes widened when she glanced at the papers on the table as she sat down. "I'm sure you recognize those," I practically growled. "Those are the non-disclosure agreements that you signed when you started working here. You violated every single clause in that document when you hired someone else to do your fucking work for you. Did you really think that I wouldn't find out?"

"She's lying," Darleen spat instantly. "She's just a home-less whore that I paid to run a few errands. If she told you that she's been doing everything, she's lying. She just wants to drive a wedge between us, baby."

Baby? I shuddered. "Funny. The first words out of her mouth were to protect you. When I read her emails on your computer, I lured her here thinking that she was a corporate spy or the press. She wanted to protect you, yet here you are blaming her for everything. I saw the documents that you sent her, Darleen. I read every single email. I even asked to see the text messages, but Julie said she deleted them. I could get a court order for them, you know. I could sue you for everything that you have."

Her face crumpled, and crocodile tears rolled down her face. I didn't buy the act for a minute. "I did it for you, baby. You were always stressed out, and you were giving me too much work, but I couldn't say no because you're so important to me. I just wanted to give you some peace of mind. I won't ever do it again. I promise."

"No," I said coldly as I stood. "You won't because you're fired. I've hired Julie to take your place, and in the week that she's been here, she's done the job far better and faster than you ever did. Get out of my sight, Darleen."

I thought that she would take the hint and leave, but it turns out that I underestimated Darleen Mason. She stood, and the fake tears were gone. Instead, her face was dark and stormy, and when she opened her mouth, she threw a temper tantrum for the ages.

"Fired?" she shrieked. "Do you have any idea what I've put up with in the past year? You are the coldest and most self-controlled man that I have ever met! You've got a stick so far up your ass that you get pissy if even one sock is out-of-place in your sock drawer. You can't for a single second just relax and smile. I don't even understand how you've never once hit on me. I think you're fucking gay, and the women on your arm are just for show. You replaced me with a whore so poor that she couldn't even afford groceries when she answered my ad. She practically kissed me, she was so grateful for work. She's the type of woman who will get knocked up and handcuff you for the next eighteen years. Mark my words, you are going to rue the day you chose her over me."

I was about to show Darleen just what happened when

I lost control, but a moving shadow caught my eye. Turning my head, I saw an unmistakable mop of blond hair. "Tyler," I growled. "What the hell are you doing here?"

Darleen whirled around, but I moved quickly and blocked her view. I was not about to have her harass Julie's kid. "Leave," I hissed at her. "Before I call the police."

She shot me one last angry look before she turned and flounced away. I could practically feel the steam rolling off her, and I had a bad feeling that it wasn't over. Turning, I looked down at the child with a frown. "Tyler?"

"You said a bad word," he pointed out. "But she said worse."

"You didn't answer my question."

He ducked his head, and I could see that the stitches had been removed. "I'm supposed to be hiding from you because Crystal is gone, and Momma didn't think you'd be happy to know that I was here. I was doing a good job too, but that woman screamed so loud, and I just had to get a look at her."

Unable to help myself, I chuckled. Trust Darleen's temper tantrum to pique a child's interest. "So you've been hiding from me all morning, huh? Where have you been?"

"Mr. Daniel said I could play in the garden, but when it got hot, he told me to come inside. Ms. Sarah gave me a couple of muffins, and Mr. Daniel told me to watch some television, but I don't really watch television, so I was exploring and pretending that I was on a top-secret mission."

Now his butler and cook were conspiring against him? Wonderful. "And what was the top-secret mission?"

"To find my daddy."

He whispered the last bit as if it was a secret, and it

wasn't the first time that I wondered about his father. "Your mother doesn't talk about him?"

Tyler shook his head. "I don't want to ask her because I think it might make her sad, and I don't want her to be sad. She cries sometimes when she thinks that I'm sleeping."

The kid had a heart of gold. He'd never make it in the world if someone didn't give him a firm hand. "I think you've been hiding long enough. Come on, let's go find your mother."

"She'll be mad."

"She won't," I promised. "It'll be okay."

To my surprise, the boy slipped his hand in mine, and I had no choice but to lead him into the house. It felt strange to hold his hand, not because his hands were so tiny but because I simply didn't hold hands with people. "I like your house," he said conversationally. "Our room is kind of small, and the sign buzzes at night."

"The sign?"

"Uh-huh. The egg sign outside our motel."

My heart squeezed in my chest. They were living at the Sunny Side Motel? Good God, the woman was living at a hooker motel? What the hell else didn't I know about Julie Dennings?

"Are you a prince? Is this your castle?"

"Believe me, I'm no one's prince," I said darkly as I stopped at the open door. At the sound of my voice, Julie looked up, and I could see the resignation on her face.

"Tyler, are you okay?" she asked softly as she tucked a strand of hair behind her ear. I couldn't help but notice that her first thought was of her son and not about her job.

"I'm sorry, Momma, but the woman was shrieking, and I just had to see her."

"Darleen." I quietly filled her in on the details, and she

pressed her lips together. I could see the wheels in her head turning as she tried to figure out what to do next.

"I know that we never talked about having my son here, and I should have asked. Crystal is out of town today and tonight, and I don't know anyone else to watch him."

It was not okay that she brought her child into work with her, and it was even worse that she didn't tell me about it, but when I spoke, I didn't tell her any of that. "It's okay. Just let me know next time, and I'll make arrangements so that he can be entertained here while you work."

Her mouth fell open in surprise, and I knew exactly how she felt. I was fairly surprised myself. "Thank you," she muttered.

"Have dinner with me tonight." What was wrong with me? Every single word out of my mouth today had a goddamn mind of its own. "A working dinner. I have a few things that I'd like to discuss with you."

"Crystal won't be back until the morning," she said, and I watched, fascinated, as her chest flushed. Everything she felt was so openly written on her face and in her body language. I'd never seen anything like it.

Tyler tugged at my hand. "I can stay here," he whispered. "Mr. Daniel promised me popcorn and movies next time I came over."

"There you go," I said simply. "Tyler will gorge himself on popcorn and animated movies while we're gone."

I could see the hesitation in her face, but she nodded. "Great. I'll make reservations at Terrence tonight."

"Terrence?" Her eyes widened. "I don't have anything to wear at a place like that."

"I'll take care of that as well. Daniel will have everything that you need when you finish." I checked my watch. "I'll be back to pick you up seven."

Releasing Tyler's hand, I left the room before she could protest even further. I knew I should be concerned about having a child in the house, but I also knew that Julie wouldn't let it affect her work. This was my one chance to get Julie out of those ridiculous cut-off shorts and into something worthy of her.

7

———

JULIE

*A*s soon as I saw the dress laying on the bed, I should have said no. The slinky black fabric with its sexy slit was something I might have worn five years ago, and I knew it would only spell disaster.

Still, I slipped it on. It had built-in cups which kept me from having to wear my bra and tuck the straps in, but it was tight enough for my panty lines to show, and my own mother taught me that panty lines under a black dress were a grave sin. So I pulled them off and tucked them beneath my folded shorts and shirt.

I had no business going to dinner with Graham Porter. I had no business wearing this dress for Graham Porter, and I certainly had no business going out to dinner without a stitch of underwear on.

I wore no make-up, and the best I could do with my hair was to wet it slightly in the bathroom and run my fingers through it to loosen the tangles. When I checked my reflection in the mirror, my heart sank. God knows how much money Graham spent on this dress, and I looked like a child playing dress-up. He even had a pair of pumps waiting for me.

The grandfather clock struck seven, and I squared my shoulders. It shouldn't have mattered to me what I looked like. This was supposed to be a business dinner and nothing more. Graham spent the past week ignoring me, and that should have been a clear sign. Despite the kiss and heavy flirtation in those first few days, he wasn't interested in a woman with a kid and a mountain of trouble. My fantasies about tonight were far grander than reality.

As I descended down the main stairwell, the front door opened, and he stepped inside. For a moment, I froze, terrified of what he would think when he looked at me, but when he did raise his head, his face was expressionless.

"I don't carry make-up with me," I said in a soft voice as I hurried down the stairs. It was way too awkward to keep walking down like I was going to make a grand entrance. "The dress and shoes fit well. You've got a good eye for that kind of thing. I'll make sure not to spill anything on it."

"Julie," he said in a low voice.

"I'll keep it in pristine shape for the next woman," I said as my tongue grew thick in my mouth. I was rambling, but I couldn't stop. "Tyler is happily watching movies with your staff. They seem happy enough to spend the night with him, but I know it's probably keeping them from their evening plans."

"Julie."

"He's had a very exciting day, so he'll pass out soon. I doubt he'll keep them up much longer."

"You look lovely."

He reached out to touch my hair, and my nervous banter immediately stopped. "I feel pretty." *Lord, please tell me that did not just come out of my mouth.* What was wrong with me? I was acting like a fifteen-year-old about to go on her first date. I expected him to snort in derision, but he just smiled.

"Good. I'm glad."

Not a date. This is not a date. This is not a date.

I chanted the words in my head for the entire drive to the restaurant, and I chanted them some more as we sat down at the elegantly dressed table. White cloth. Lit candles. Sparkling wine glasses.

"This is not a date," I blurted out suddenly. The hostess stopped short of putting the menu down, and I cringed. I was wrong. I wasn't acting like a fifteen-year-old. The fifteen-year-old me would have been much smoother in this situation. I more resembled a babbling idiot.

"Just leave the menus, thank you," Graham said as he nodded his head. The young and pretty hostess giggled before doing as he asked and sauntering away. "Are you a red or white wine drinker?"

"I'm a water drinker. Sometimes cola if I'm feeling daring. Of course, I usually have some juice and milk in the house." *Stop talking.* "Either is fine. I've enjoyed both."

He set the wine menu down and frowned at me. "Julie, I didn't ask you out tonight to talk about work, but this isn't meant to be romance and flowers. I don't do dates. What I did want to do was treat you to a nice dinner and help you relax a little. When was the last time you were out with a man?"

The night Jonathan took me out to a waterside restaurant with just as much glamour and romance as this restaurant and asked for my engagement ring back. "Five years."

"Tyler's father?"

Oh, I so did not want to talk about that. "Yes. I feel like after everything you've done for me, I should be taking you out to dinner."

Graham was apparently not going to let me off the hook that easily. "Why is Tyler's father no longer in the picture?"

I had several choices. I could tell him the truth, but I wasn't willing to trust Tyler's well-being to Graham Porter. I could ignore the question, but then he'd just do his own digging. I could tell him mostly the truth, making it sound as boring as possible, and hope that he loses interest.

I chose option three.

"It's not a new story," I said with a shrug as I leaned back. "Jonathan and I had a whirlwind romance. He swept me off my feet and told me everything that I wanted to hear. Unfortunately, I found out that he wasn't the man of my dreams. Things ended badly, and shortly after, I discovered that I was pregnant. I didn't want Jonathan in my life anymore, so I chose not to tell him."

"He could have supported you financially. Helped you out."

Stiffening my back, I clenched my fists under the table. "I don't need any help with my son."

I knew that I sounded like a mother lion, but Graham didn't back down. "He never found out?"

"I thought this dinner was supposed to relax me?"

"I'm just trying to figure you out, Julie. You're a hard woman to get to know. Usually women are throwing themselves at me, but I kiss you once and you don't even want to be in the same room as me."

Remembering that kiss sent waves of heat through me. "That wasn't a romantic kiss," I reminded him.

"It wasn't meant to be." He cocked his head. "But it was heated none-the-less, and I'd be lying if I didn't admit that I've been thinking of doing it again and again."

I needed a distraction. Any distraction. A fire in the kitchen would have been wonderful. Where the hell was our waiter? "You were the one who disappeared for a week."

"Just trying to stay away from temptation." His smooth voice sent delicious shivers down my spine, and I ached in places that I shouldn't be aching. Not wearing panties was making things very uncomfortable.

"We can't."

"We can, Julie. As long as you aren't looking for a happily-ever-after kind of ending, we can have all the fun we want. I promise that you'll enjoy every single second of it."

I didn't doubt that. "I work for you."

"So I won't touch you during work hours."

"My son."

"I'll give you a nice, long lunch break."

"Welcome to Terrance!" The chipper voice broke whatever spell I was under, and I jumped as if she'd just poured cold water on me. "My name is Jenny, and I'll be taking care of you. Can I get you started with a bottle of Chateau St. James Merlot or perhaps a La Prima Chardonnay?"

Graham smoothly ordered something that I'd never heard of before and sent her on her way. "Where were we?" he asked with a lazy smile.

Feeling more in control, I picked up the menu. "I was just about to ask you what's good here. I'm famished."

He didn't object to my sudden change in subject, and even though we kept the conversation running smoothly through dinner, I knew that he wasn't finished with me just yet.

Sure enough, when he slipped into the driver's seat of his car and pulled away from the valet station of the restaurant, his hand settled on the bare skin of my thigh just above my knee. I could have pushed it away, but it had been a long time since a man had touched me, and I just couldn't do it. When he pulled into the drive and parked in front of the mansion, I noticed that no one came out to greet us. We were completely alone, and his hand slid up higher.

"I knew it," he muttered in a thick voice. "No panties."

"Graham," I whispered.

"I'll never make you do anything that you don't want to do, Julie. Say the word, and I'll never touch you again."

His words lingered in the air, and I knew that he had to feel the heat emanating from my center. Just a touch higher, and he'd find out just how much I wanted him. I should have said no. Getting involved with a man like Graham Porter would not end well, but I was already too far gone, and when I widened my legs, he groaned and caressed his fingers over my slick folds.

Pleasure shot through me, and I jumped, but he was already leaning over the console. Just like before, the kiss wasn't gentle. Instead, it held the promise of everything that he might do to me.

"Wait," I gasped. "Tyler is waiting for me."

With a groan, he pulled away and rested his forehead against mine. "You're killing me," he said hoarsely.

"I'm sorry." His fingers moved ever so gently against my sensitive clit, and I moaned. "Graham, you've got to stop, or I'm going to lose my mind. I want you, but I can't do this in the car when my son is waiting for me inside."

"You're right," he sighed. "I need more room to maneuver anyway, and I want to be able to take my time with you. Find out just what makes you moan."

Scrambling for the handle of the car, I practically fell out. If I didn't get away from him now, I'd end up straddling him in his ridiculously expensive car and making a mess all over his leather seats.

Not bothering to look back, I hurried up the steps. Daniel opened the door and smiled. "Ms. Dennings. We all had a wonderful time with Tyler tonight. He's a brilliant child."

Afraid that the butler might know what we were up to, I smoothed my hands nervously through my hair. "I appreciate you looking after him. Is he asleep?"

"Yes, ma'am. He fell asleep about an hour ago in the downstairs guestroom."

"Thank you." I tried to compose myself as I walked swiftly to his room. The door was cracked open, and there was a soft nightlight illuminating his sleeping form. Sitting down by the bed, I smoothed my hand over his hair and gently woke him up.

"Hi, baby," I whispered. "Are you ready to go home?"

"Hi, Momma. Can we stay here tonight? I'm so tired, and the sign keeps me awake at night."

Pain squeezed my chest. I thought that he slept through the night, but obviously I was wrong. Would Graham let us spend the night? "Of course, baby. Let me talk to Mr. Porter, and then I'll come sleep next to you, okay?"

He wrinkled his nose. "I'm not a baby, Momma. There are plenty of other bedrooms."

Chuckling, I kissed the top of his head. "It's a strange house, Tyler. What if you get scared in the middle of the night?"

"Mr. Daniel taught me how to use the iPad on the wall if I need anything. And I won't get scared. I like this house. He says that in the morning, he'll teach me to make donuts. Can I make donuts?"

Great. My four-year-old was enjoying the lap of luxury. That's just what every poverty-stricken mother wanted to hear. "Sure, baby. That sounds fun." He settled back in the bed, and I tucked the covers around him and stayed until his breathing evened out. Quietly, I slipped out of his room.

Graham was waiting for me. "He wanted to spend the night," I said as I took a deep breath. "I hope that's okay."

"That's fine." His voice was even, but his eyes were anything but. "I assume that you'll be sleeping with him?"

"I thought that as well, but he seemed insulted by the idea. I can just sleep on the couch or maybe grab one of the spare rooms upstairs."

Before I could stop him, Graham slipped into Tyler's room. I watched silently as he did something to the iPad before quietly walking out and closing the door behind him. "The tablet can work as a monitor. If he wakes up in the middle of the night, we'll know about it."

"We?"

Graham took my hand and pulled me towards him. When his lips settled on mine, I had nothing left to argue. Tonight, I would be his.

Breaking off the kiss, he led me up the stairs. My senses whirled as I climbed each step. Since the moment Tyler was born, I hadn't had much time to think of myself sexually. For the first two years, I was too exhausted to think of doing anything else that would keep me from sleep, and in the next two years, I'd stopped thinking of myself as a sexual being altogether.

Graham had awakened something in me that I could barely remember. I felt sexual. Powerful. Feminine.

Opening the door to his bedroom, he pulled me in and pushed me up against the wall as he kissed me again. His tongue thrust inside, hot and demanding, and my knees weakened. I could feel his hard erection against my belly, and all I could do was wrap my arms around his neck and hang on.

"What do you like, Julie?" he whispered, his breath hot in my ear. "Tell me what you like."

I liked whatever the hell his tongue was doing to my ear. "Don't stop," I pleaded.

"That's not an answer, sweetheart. Has it been so long that you've forgotten?" He picked up my hand and kissed the inside of my wrist. My senses came alive, and I gasped at the spikes of pleasure.

He laughed, low and throaty. "I guess you like that. Let's see what else makes you moan." His lips were on my neck, kissing and sucking as he worked the zipper of my dress down. It cascaded down my body and pooled to the floor leaving me to the mercy of his questing hands.

They slid up my naked sides, caressing, teasing, and I couldn't do anything but tremble under his touch. I wanted him just as naked, but if I let go, I'd slide bonelessly to the floor.

"Graham," I cried out as his fingers reached my nipples. "I'm going to fall."

"I won't let that happen." Before I knew what was happening, he'd picked me up and nuzzled the crook of my neck as he carried me to his bed. When he reached for the lamp by the bed, I grabbed his arm.

"Don't." Surrounded by luxury, I could only imagine how plain I would look. I wanted to keep this in the dark where I could pretend that I belonged in his bed, even if just for the night.

He moved, his face catching the moonlight. "I want to see you."

"Not now. Just fuck me. Please."

Something changed in him when I begged him. His face hardened, and he suddenly left me. Bewildered, I raised myself up on my elbows and listened to his clothes rustling in the dark. "Graham?"

"I'm here." His voice was almost cold as he covered my body, and bit my bottom lip.

"Did I say something to upset you? I'm sorry."

"Stop apologizing for everything, Julie. Just lie back and enjoy." I wanted to ask him what I'd done wrong, but his fingers were on the inside of my thigh, and all my insecurities fled. He stroked me and played me until I sang for him, and all the while, I touched him. His skin was smooth and warm under my touch, but his muscles were taut with restraint. I reveled in the feel of him, all that power inside one man. He wanted me to relax, and I just wanted him to lose just a fraction of that cold control.

When I wrapped my hands around his cock, he hissed in the dark, and I smiled as I squeezed.

"Fuck, Julie," he groaned. "You keep that up, and it'll be over before it begins."

He reached across me to the nightstand, and I heard him rip the foil. It took him only seconds before he was over me again, his lips on mine and his thumb circling my clit. Tension built inside me as he pressed and circled and released, and it wasn't until I was on the edge of chaos that he slammed into me with a hoarse cry.

Pain and pleasure ripped through me, and I let out a strangled moan. "Oh, God," I hissed.

"Fuck, Julie." He froze over me and gasped. "Baby, you're so tight. Why didn't you tell me? I didn't mean to hurt you."

Why was he stopping? I wiggled my hips under him, and he exhaled a shuddering breath. "You've got to stop moving, sweetheart. Give yourself a minute. I can't hold out much longer...ah...goddammit!"

His control snapped, and he withdrew and thrust. Wrapping my legs around him, I cried out as my first orgasm broke, a wave of pleasure cresting through me. He knew, and flicked my nipples and licked my skin until I was flying high again. Each thrust was more powerful than the last, and the entire bed shook as he pounded inside me. I could barely breathe as he controlled every inch of my body, and when I shattered again, he buried his face in the crook of my shoulder and cried out my name as he came with me.

8

JULIE

"Are you okay?" He rolled off my body and disposed of the condom. His hand rested lightly on my abdomen, but there was no cuddling involved. I tried to tell myself that it was fine. This was just about sex and nothing else. "When you said it had been a few years since you'd been on a date, I didn't realize that meant sex as well."

"I've never had casual sex," I admitted. "So this will be a first for me. Mostly my abstinence was because of Tyler. As a single mother, I'd usually choose sleep over sex. I'm okay though. The pain didn't last long."

"There shouldn't have been any pain at all," he growled in my ear. "You need to tell me these things, Julie."

I chuckled humorlessly and rolled to face him. In the moonlight, I could see the hard lines of his face and the anger in his eyes. "I usually wait until the third week of meeting someone before I talk freely about my sex life."

"Tell me about your family."

I wanted to ask him why. My family wasn't exactly pillow talk, but he maneuvered me until I was curled up against his chest. His fingers lightly stroked my back, and in that moment, I was happy. Stroking his skin, I smiled.

"I grew up in Texas. No siblings and two doting parents, so I was a fairly spoiled brat. My father worked for some huge corporation, and my Momma was a stay-at-home parent. When Daddy got a promotion, we moved around a lot. For the next eight years, we lived in five different states. I threw a fit each time. It got to the point where I didn't even bother trying to make friends or date. It was a hard life, but my parents did the best they could."

He kissed the top of my head, and I sighed. "I'd applied to some colleges around the country, but I had my heart set on going to school in Florida. I wanted sun and sand and romance. A month before I was set to move, Daddy had a heart attack. He died before they could even get him to the hospital, and my momma fell apart. Over the next year, I watched her wither away to practically nothing. They told me that she probably had a blood clot, but I just knew that she'd died of a broken heart. It wasn't until I was dealing with the funeral that I realized we were broke. I'd never thought we were rich, but I always thought we had plenty of money. I'd assumed they were going to pay for my college, and they never denied me anything."

Closing my eyes, I rested on his chest, listening to the beat of his heart. "What happened next?" he prompted.

"I don't want to talk about that," I muttered.

"Why not?"

"Because you already know. There was nothing left. I started working as a bartender to make some money so I could live, and then Jonathan swooped into my life. The rest, as they say, is history."

"Just tell me, Julie. Is it really so hard for you to open up to someone, or is it just so hard for you to open up to me?"

I popped my head up and glared at him. "Talking is a two-way street, you know. I don't see you volunteering any information about your family."

He grinned and flashed those perfect white teeth. "My story is about the same as every other rich kid. My parents ignored me. Daniel raised me. Then, when I was in college, the family jet crashed in the mountains and pretty much took out the whole family. It's just me and my cousin Miles now."

"That's it?" I demanded. "That's all you've got to say?"

"I wasn't raised with love, Julie. I was raised to be more concerned about what my peers thought of me than what I thought of myself. I was taught to care about my family's reputation more than I needed to care about my family. That makes my life pretty boring."

"You never rebelled? Not once?"

"You tell me about Tyler's birth, and I'll tell you about the one time I did rebel."

One time, my ass. Still, I settled back down and tried to remember the worst year of my life. "There was a free clinic by my apartment. They weren't really equipped to handle pregnancies, but they monitored me the best that they could. I had some things that I could pawn in order to pay for the hospital bill, and I worked until the night that I gave birth. I think God must have pitied me because he gave me the best baby. It wasn't a walk in the park, but I was only in labor for four hours before he popped out. He didn't even cry, which nearly gave me a heart attack, but he was as healthy as healthy could be."

I smiled at the memory. "I took one look at his face, and I knew that I would walk to Hell and back to make that little boy happy. I named him after my father, and I wrapped him up and took him home. The clinic had gathered a few things for me, and I'd bought pretty much everything else used. He wasn't really a crier, nor was he a troublemaker, but he loved to explore. I'd take my eyes away from him for a minute, and he'd toddle off to check something else out."

Graham grunted. "I guess he likes to explore trees too."

I shuddered, remembering that day at the hospital. "He's a stubborn boy. It's hard to tell him that he can't do something. Now you tell me about rebelling."

Tangling his fingers in my hair, he shook his head. "You're not done yet. Did you ever tell Jonathan about Tyler?"

"I sent word to him. He never responded," I lied. The truth still hurt too much to say out loud.

"And why do you keep moving around?"

"Restless. I guess I didn't hate moving around as much as I thought I did." Yet another lie. It was a good thing we weren't planning on a serious relationship, or I'd have quite a bit of explaining to do. "Now tell me your story."

"I was eighteen," he said in a low voice. "And I was in love with the most beautiful girl. She went to the community college here, and she didn't have a quarter to her name. We wouldn't have ever met except that Miles was dating some friend of hers and introduced us at a party. I saw her in secret for about a month, and when my parents found out, they threatened to disinherit me. I think it was the only time I'd ever seen them show any kind of emotion."

"Disinherit? Just for dating a girl?" I gasped. "Really?"

"Well, it may have been more than that," he admitted. "The truth was that I wanted to marry her. I'd asked my mother for my grandmother's ring to give to her."

"After just a month?" The words were out of my mouth before I could stop them. Who was I to judge? I'd dated

Jonathan for all of three months before he slipped a ring on my finger.

"I was so in love with her that I didn't even care. I told my parents that I didn't give a damn about their money, and I drove that night to see her. I told her what happened, and I swore that I'd find a way to take care of her."

I tried to picture a teenage Graham slinging drinks for a living to help support his girlfriend. The image almost made me giggle. "How romantic."

"She didn't see it that way." His voice grew cold and distant. "She told me that I needed to patch things up with my parents. I thought at first she cared about me and my family, but then she said that she couldn't be with me unless I was going to inherit their wealth, and I knew right then that she was only after me for my money."

What a horrible story. "Graham." My heart broke for him. "You were so young."

"Yes, but it was a lesson that I needed to learn. My parents already knew that."

I was about to remind him that not everyone was out for his money when he gripped my hips and pulled me up. As my knees fell apart on either side of him, I felt his hard cock probing at my entrance.

"That made you hard?" I gasped.

"You make me hard," he admitted. "Everything about you. From the damn way you bite your bottom lip to those ridiculous tattered jean shorts. From the moment I laid eyes on you, all I could think about was how it would feel to slip inside you and fuck you until you came."

Wet heat pooled between my thighs at his words, and I rocked along the length of him. "I know what you mean," I whispered. "I wanted you to fuck me on the desk."

"Ah, God, Julie. I wish you hadn't told me that. Now I

won't be able to stop thinking about it." He filled his hands with my tiny breasts, and I tried to pull back. "Why do you keep doing that?"

"I don't know," I whispered. "You date beautiful models and actresses. I just don't feel..." my voice trailed off as my cheeks burned with embarrassment.

"I don't date anyone," he said gruffly. "I escort wealthy and beautiful women to parties, and yes, sometimes I bring them home, but I don't date anyone. And believe me, not the first one of them has driven me crazy the way that you have, Julie. I think that you may be the most genuine woman I've ever met."

And yet half the words that came out of my mouth was a lie. "You should meet new people."

"And you should ride me right now." He reached over and tossed something my way. The foil of another condom glinted in the moonlight as I caught it. It had been awhile since I dressed a man, but I remembered a few things.

When I touched the tip of my tongue to the underside of his cock, he inhaled sharply. I had every intention of riding him until I was screaming his name in the dark, but I wanted to tease him just a bit first. I wrapped my hand around his cock and squeezed as I slipped my mouth over him.

"Fuck, Julie," he cried out hoarsely. "Suck my cock, sweetheart."

"You like that?" I asked with a husky laugh before I took him even deeper. His hands were tangled in my hair, but he didn't push or pull. He just let me go at my own pace until he was jerking me off him.

"Minx," he hissed. I laughed and fumbled with the condom. Sliding it on him. I straddled his hips and slowly lowered myself on him.

My muscles still felt a little sore, but as he thrust inside me, I didn't care. The angle was deeper, harder, and his fingers dug into my hips as he forced me up and down. In and out. I was powerless to regain control, and when I finally fell across his chest and he hammered inside me, all I could do was whimper.

"Say my name," he swore. "I want to hear my name on your lips when you come. I want you to know who's making your body burn. Come on, Julie, sweetheart. Come with me. I'm right here."

He slid across that sweet spot, and I complied with a hoarse scream. His name cut through the dark, and when his own orgasm joined mine, I fell heavily on top of him and rode the wave of mind-blowing pleasure until sleep claimed me.

9

———

GRAHAM

*J*ulie was still sleeping when I woke up, and I didn't have the heart to interrupt her rest. It had only been a few hours since I'd woken her up and taken her again. It was insane how I couldn't seem to slake my lust for her. Just staring at her vulnerable beauty, her hair fanned out across my pillow, my cock hardened once again for her. If she knew just how exposed she was in the daylight, she'd probably hide under the covers, so I had my fill looking at her. After last night, I'd memorized her body by touch, and this morning, I drank her in.

Genuine. Untouched. Perfect.

The thoughts didn't sit well with me, so I eased from the bed. I needed to put some space between us. Throwing on a pair of boxers, I padded across the carpet to the tablet on the wall and checked my messages. The house was quiet.

Quietly slipping out of the room, I checked on the guest room downstairs. It was empty, but I could hear the soft sound of a child's laughter drifting from the kitchen. Following it, I saw Daniel and Sarah standing around the stove while Tyler sat on the countertop. I already knew what they were doing. It was what Daniel used to do with me every Sunday morning.

Fry donuts.

"I guess a healthy breakfast is out of the question," I said wryly as I headed to the counter to pour myself a cup of coffee.

"Good morning, Mr. Porter," Tyler said cheerfully. "Do you like donuts?"

Daniel snorted, and I ignored him. "I used to, but it's been a while. Call me Graham. I'm not old enough to be Mr. Porter yet. Did you sleep well?"

"I did. Have you seen my momma?"

Sarah turned around and glared at me. It wasn't like the older woman to disapprove of my sexual partners, but I knew that Tyler was worming his way into their hearts. It would only be a matter of time before the child had every member of my staff wrapped around his finger.

"I think she's still sleeping," I said carefully. "Do you want me to get her for you?"

"No. She needs her sleep," he said in all seriousness. "I think the sign keeps her up too."

That blasted motel sign. I needed to get them out of that room as quickly as possible. "It must be. Have you been up long?"

Tyler shook his head. "No. I told Mr. Daniel that we couldn't eat a big breakfast. It's Sunday, and Momma takes me on a picnic on Sundays."

"A picnic, huh? Where do you guys picnic?"

"Last week we went to Burger King."

Burger King? Confused, I stared at him. "You went for a picnic at Burger King?"

Enthusiastically, the kid nodded. "Uh-huh. We'd go

through the drive-thru and then park somewhere nice and eat."

Julie was one hell of a mother. There wasn't a doubt in my mind that Tyler asked her for a picnic one day, not having a clue what it meant, and she did the best that she could under the circumstances. "You know, I used to have picnics too, but we did things a bit differently."

"Really? What did you do?"

"We used to pack a lunch in a basket and go eat out in the gardens. We'd play card games or fly kites. Sometimes we'd play tag." I was talking out of my ass. I knew what other families did during picnics, but no Porter would be caught dead eating outside unless it was on some fancy patio where the glass of champagne cost more than the meal.

Tyler's eyes rounded at the thought. "Really? That sounds like fun. Momma, can we try that?"

Turning slowly, I saw Julie frozen in the doorway. She was dressed in the outfit she'd worn yesterday, and I could see the anger in her eyes. She obviously didn't like me putting ideas in Tyler's head. "I'd be more than happy to take you two on a picnic for lunch," I said softly. I had a million things that I needed to do, but if I could make that kid and his mother smile, I was going to do that first.

She didn't look like she wanted to smile, but she forced one anyway as she stared at Tyler. "Let's see if you have room for lunch first," she said tightly. "Those donuts sure do smell good. Let's go straighten up your room first, okay?"

"That's not necessary," Daniel and I said together, but Tyler hopped off the counter.

"Yes," Julie said firmly. "It is necessary. Tyler needs to learn how to be a proper guest."

As she left, Daniel and Sarah both glowered at me.

Despite the fact that Daniel raised me, he was my servant, and I knew that he wouldn't say anything to me, but Sarah was another story entirely. The older woman, with her robust figure and greying hair, was one of the most outspoken people I knew.

"You have no business with that woman," she snapped. "She is your employee and a struggling single mother to boot. You are just waiting to break her heart."

"Sarah," Daniel growled. "How many times do I have to tell you to keep your opinions to yourself?"

She didn't look the least bit sorry. "You feel the exact same way. You all but told me that when we woke up this morning." She immediately reddened. "I mean, when I saw you this morning."

I knew that Daniel and Sarah had something going on, but this was the first time that I had proof. I was happy for them. For as long as I'd known Daniel, I'd never seen him with a woman. "I'll try not to comment on your relationship if you refrain from commenting on mine," I said dryly.

"So you're going to admit that it's a relationship and not a one-night stand?" she snapped.

"Your donuts are burning," I said easily as I stood. "I have some phone calls to make this morning. Please inform Julie and her son that they are welcome to enjoy the recreation areas of the house. If they wish, see to it that you pack them a nice picnic lunch. I'm sure I can spare an hour for a brief repast."

I was well into my first conference call when Daniel messaged me to tell me that Julie and Tyler had decided to stay for a picnic. Part of me wanted her to leave so I didn't have to deal with the day-after emotions, and part of me was already needing to fill her again. There was no doubt in my mind that had Tyler not said that he wanted a picnic, Julie would not still be here.

Why the hell had I offered to take them on a picnic? I'd never been on one in my entire life. I was supposed to be creating distance between myself and Julie, not giving her excuses to hang around.

There was another message from Miles. He wanted to know how the confrontation with Darleen went, but I ignored it. The last thing I wanted to do was explain that I'd hired Julie and bedded her within a week of her working for me.

The investment call ran much longer that I'd anticipated because an unexpected voice on the other end was Reid Foster, a Stonecutters fraternity brother from my college days. The friendly rivalry between the two of us that had us competing in drinking games at our exclusive rich-boy-frat-parties back then had us negotiating over percentage points today. I'd barely scratched off my to-do list when Daniel messaged me again to tell me that Julie and Tyler were waiting.

Trying to stow my irritation, after all, it was my idea, I unbuttoned the top buttons of my shirt and headed down the stairs. Tyler took one look at me and immediately frowned. "Why are you so dressed up? I thought we were going to the garden."

"Tyler!" Julie shushed him, but I could see the same question in her eyes as well. "There's no need to join us if you're busy."

It was on the tip of my tongue to suggest that they go without me, but I craved her nearness. Work was forgotten the minute that unhappy line creased her forehead. All I wanted to do was kiss her and tell her that there was nothing more I wanted to do.

"I have to eat as well," I said with a stiff smile. "And I promise that I can play just as easily in these clothes as I could in something else." Not to mention that I didn't really own any casual clothes. My life didn't really require it.

Sarah glared at me as she handed me the picnic basket. I thanked her, but she ignored me as she bent down and ruffled Tyler's hair. As she told him to have a good time, I realized that my staff was rebelling against me.

How could they judge me when they clearly liked Julie and Tyler as much as I did? Did it really matter that we wanted them for two different reasons?

Tyler chatted incessantly about their morning activities as we walked to the gardens. There were picnic tables, but Sarah had packed a blanket, and Tyler insisted that we spread it out on the ground. I realized how much we must have looked like a happy family to any passerby's, and I found it difficult to breathe.

"Graham? Do you want chicken salad or tuna salad?" Julie asked as she pulled out the two containers. "Sarah also packed a peanut butter and jelly sandwich, but I think Tyler might wrestle you for it."

My stomach turned as I stared at her. "I'm not hungry," I muttered.

Julie turned her head and watched Tyler scamper through the flowers. "This was a mistake," she said softly. "I should never have agreed to this."

"To what? It's just lunch." Hadn't I said that before?

"It's not just lunch," she snapped. "Tyler is getting attached to you, and that's dangerous. He's getting to that age where he's going to want to have a father figure around, and we both know where this is going."

Her words were like a slap in the face. All at once, I saw her face in the bed last night. I'd wanted to lave attention on her, and she just wanted to be fucked. "Where is this going?"

"You got what you wanted last night. I figured I'd be lucky if I kept my job for another week before you found some reason to let me go. This is not stable, and with all the instability in Tyler's life, I can't have him thinking that you're going to be sticking it out."

I clenched my jaw. "Are you telling me that you wanted to fuck me so bad that you were willing to lose your job over it?"

She inhaled sharply, but before she could reply, Tyler had returned. "Mr. Porter, there's a man coming to join us."

Whipping my head around, I saw Miles crossing the lawn towards us. He was grinning like a fool, and I knew the only thing that could make this situation worse was if he got involved.

"That's my cousin," I said as I stood. "I wasn't expecting him. You two enjoy your picnic. If I can't rejoin you, I'll try to make it up to you."

To his credit, Tyler didn't complain as I walked away, and Julie never said a word. All I could think about was how many times my own father had promised me something only to fail to follow through.

"Did you get yourself a wife and kid while I was gone?" Miles asked as I joined him. "Flat chest, but damn, look at the curves on her hips."

I didn't think twice as I pulled my elbow back and sent my fist smashing into his jaw.

10

———

JULIE

Just as I suspected, I didn't even see Graham in the coming week. Although he texted me regularly, he never said a word about the night we spent together or the terrible day afterward. I wasn't surprised when he left the picnic early, although I was annoyed that he even suggested it to begin with. What wasn't tolerated was the violent punch that he'd thrown right in front of Tyler. I was so angry that I couldn't even look back at him as I gathered the picnic things and hurried away.

Tyler was a flurry of questions, and I couldn't answer a single one of them. It took all afternoon to finally get him settled, and then I had to hide from Crystal to avoid her questions.

There was a simple note the next morning with a list of things he wanted me to do. At the very end were two simple words.

I'm sorry.

Graham didn't seem like a man who apologized easily,

and I couldn't figure out what he was apologizing for. Was he saying that he never should have touched me? That he initiated contact with my son? That he left us in the middle of everything?

I didn't have the nerve to ask. I was ashamed to admit that even though I was angry, and even though I knew it would never end well, I missed his touch. I missed his lips on mine, the feel over his body pressed against mine, the way he took the time to learn everything I liked.

I was in way over my head.

"Miss, you can't come in here! Miss!"

At the sound of Daniel's frantic voice, I snapped my head up. Before I could even rise from my desk, the door flew open and those telltale heels clicked across the hard-wood floor. "You fucked him, didn't you!" Darleen shrieked.

"I'm so sorry," Daniel gasped as he chased after her. "I guess Mr. Porter forgot to revoke her access code. I'll call the police."

"Darleen, do you want Daniel to call the police?" I asked in a calm voice. "Or do you think we can sit down and discuss this like adults?"

For a moment, I thought she'd throw something at me, but she slid into the chair and crossed her arms. "I think we're fine here," I told Daniel. "I'll let you know if that changes."

"Mr. Porter will not be happy that she's here," he muttered under his breath as he walked away.

Although my voice was even, my heart was pounding something crazy. I didn't think for a single second that Darleen was sane when it came to Graham. "I want you to know that I was happy with our arrangement. I didn't mean for this to happen."

"Then you shouldn't have taken the job," she hissed.

"I need the money. You know that." I looked at the woman and felt some pity. It was obvious that she'd had her sights set on Graham, and it was just as obvious that she didn't know a thing about him. *And you do?* My inner voice taunted me, and I ignored it. "I have a son to think about."

"Were you thinking about your son when you spent the night last night? When you went to dinner with him wearing that slutty dress?"

My back stiffened. "And how would you know all that?"

"I have my sources," she said as she stuck her nose up in the air. "You know just as well as I do that you don't belong in his world. You're just some piece of trash who lives out of a motel, and he'll figure you out for the gold-digging slut that you."

Even though she hadn't raised her voice, she was getting nasty. "You don't know the first thing about me," I reminded her coldly.

"And neither does he," Darleen snapped. "Look at you. You're pathetic. You can barely take care of yourself or that creepy kid of yours, and you think sucking a rich man's cock will get you everything that you want."

"That's enough," Graham said coldly. Darleen gasped and whirled around. I hadn't even realized that he was in the house, and I'd never seen such anger in his face before. His gaze shot daggers of ice, and for a moment, I thought that perfect control of his would snap. "Get out before I throw you out."

To my surprise, Darleen didn't even seem upset as she stood. In fact, she smirked. "I'm going to remember this moment when it all comes tumbling down around you," she said as she glanced my way. When she stroked Graham's arm on the way out, I wanted to pick up the potted plant on my desk and hurl it in her direction.

"Are you okay?" he asked me when she'd walked away. "I've already had her access code revoked, so this won't happen again. I should have done it immediately."

"I'm fine, but I'm fairly certain that she's stalking you. You might want to look into that." I didn't like the concern in his eyes when he watched me. It made me feel secure, and the last thing that I needed to do was feel secure around him. "Have you been here all week?"

He leaned against the door, and I realized that there were circles under his eyes. "Yes," he said quietly.

I wanted to remind him that a vague apology on paper meant nothing, but I also wanted to keep my job. Forcing a smile, I nodded my head. "I'm sure you've been busy. I'm actually ahead of schedule today, so if you need me to do anything else, feel free to let me know."

"You're not angry?"

"Why would I be angry? This is your home, and I work for you. So long as you pay me, I don't need to concern myself with where you are." The words were almost stuck in my throat, and I had to force them out.

To my utter dismay, he stepped inside and closed the door. "Since I'm here, I'd like to talk with you about what happened."

"It's not necessary." There was no escape. "I'm perfectly happy pretending that it didn't happen."

"I'm not."

Of course he wasn't. If there was one thing that I was learning about Graham Porter, it was that he wasn't predictable in the slightest. "Very well. We can acknowledge that it happened and that it won't happen again."

He turned his head up slightly, and a sexy smile spread

across his face. "Won't it? Even right now, my body is screaming for me to touch you. Why should I ignore that?"

"Sex is complicated," I whispered.

"It doesn't have to be. We can avoid the awkward days after by avoiding spending the night together. It's a simple solution."

"If all you want is sex, I'm sure that women will be lining up outside your door for a night with you." I tried to sound bored as he sat in the chair across from me and stretched out his legs. Why did he have to be so tempting?

"They're not you, and there are things that I haven't done with you yet. I haven't tasted you. I want to slide my tongue across your clit until you scream for mercy. And I believe we already talked about your fantasy of spreading your legs for me on a desk. Was it this desk?"

Swallowing hard, I tried not to look at the desk. I kept my gaze trained on him as though I wasn't growing wet at his words or tormented by the mental images in my head. "Why me?" I whispered. "Is it just because you know you shouldn't? Is it about control?"

"My urges are a little more basic than that," he said in a low voice. "I want you, Julie. Pure and simple. It has nothing to do with anything else."

Before I could respond, there was a knock on the door and it swung open. To my surprise, the man from the garden strolled in with a cocky grin. "I'm sorry. Am I interrupting something? I was fairly certain that I heard screaming earlier, and I thought I might be missing out on all the fun."

Graham growled. "The door was closed for a reason."

"I knocked." The younger man was just as handsome as Graham, and I knew without a doubt that they were related. He winked at me as he stretched his hand out. "Graham has terrible manners, so I'll introduce myself. I'm Miles Porter.

You must be the lovely and mysterious Julie Dennings. The first time I heard your name, Graham was certain that you were up to something truly devious. If his original assumptions were correct, you're a master at worming your way into the heart of the Porter mansion."

"For God's sakes, Miles," Graham muttered. "Do you have to be such an idiot?"

I wasn't one to let another smooth talking Porter catch me off-guard. "Deception of the Porter family isn't high on my list. How's that jaw feel, by the way?" I fixed a steely look at Graham. "My son wanted to know why he wasn't allowed to punch people like that."

Graham had the decency to glance at the floor, but Miles chuckled. "I'm afraid the punch was well deserved. Graham was simply defending your honor, although I suppose we owe the boy an apology. I was looking forward to getting to know him. Daniel tells me that he's quite the charmer, and this house could use a little charm."

"I need to get back to work," Graham said suddenly as he stood. "Julie, we'll finish this conversation up at a later date. If my cousin doesn't keep you too long, you're welcome to go home early."

His voice was chilly, as if the conversation in question hadn't heated his blood the way it had heated mine. I was left puzzled as he stormed out. "Don't mind him," Miles said as he took Graham's seat. "He is emotionally stunted. It's the Porter genes. Did I miss a good catfight? I always wanted to know how Darleen would fair with those huge jugs of hers slowing her down."

The idea of Darleen and I in a knock-down-drag-out fight was so absurd that I had to laugh, although I was sure that was Miles's plan all along. I'd known him for less than ten minutes, and I already liked him. He had a way about him that made me feel at ease, and he was so different from Graham. I wondered if his parents were a little more warm and loving. "You didn't miss anything," I said easily. "Although it's been a long time since I've been in a fight, I don't think Darleen is the type who cries at a broken nail despite her prissy attitude. She'd probably surprise everyone."

Miles leaned forward, and the light caught his eyes. I realized that they had the same greyish tint that Graham's had. "You? In a fight? Do tell."

"Oh yeah," I laughed. "I took down Mark Golding with one swift kick when he tried to take my Barbie lunchbox. I saved up six months worth of allowance to buy it, and I was not about to let him get his grubby hands on it!"

Miles whistled. "One kick, huh?"

"To the groin. Works every time."

He visibly winced, and I chuckled. I wanted to spend the rest of the afternoon talking to him and maybe grilling him about Graham, but he stood and stretched. "Unfortunately, I'm not just here for pleasure, but I do want to get to know more about the woman who has made my cousin resort to violence."

"I'm sure you don't have to worry about that again," I said as a dull flush creeped up my cheeks. "It was just a bad day for everyone."

"You should get to know him," Miles said softly. "I think you might be surprised by what you find."

I was speechless when he walked away. Surely Miles knew that I wasn't the kind of woman that should be getting to know Graham, but his words echoed in my head. Maybe I had painted Graham unfairly. Just because the circumstances resembled Jonathan's didn't mean that they were two peas in a pod. Maybe I'd spent so much time protecting myself and Tyler that I didn't realize how much we were both lacking.

It sounded insane in my head, but maybe Miles was right. Maybe I should take a chance and see what Graham had to offer.

Especially since I was already half in love with the man.

11

GRAHAM

Business kept me busy for the next few days, but I couldn't stop thinking about her. She invaded my dreams when I tried to sleep and consumed my thoughts when I was awake. I'd never experienced this kind of obsession before. I wanted to press my mouth to her body until she cried out my name again, but I also wanted to hold her and ask her more questions about her life.

It put me in the worst mood, and having my cousin around didn't make things better.

"I think you made the right choice by not investing with Calloway's new business," he announced at breakfast. "It's already falling apart. Word around the water cooler is that his lovely new wife found out that he's been enjoying multiple women on the side, and she's gearing up to take half of everything he owns."

"That's what he gets for getting married," I grunted as I reached for my coffee. "And you don't have a water cooler."

"I know." He sighed. "It makes me think that we missed out on something great. Maybe we should get a water cooler. Do you think the staff will gossip around it?"

"They'll gossip about you." I had a terrible headache, and I was in no mood to listen to his banter. "What the hell are you doing here?"

"I finalized the paperwork for the condos yesterday, but I've missed you, Graham. I thought I might stick around and see how you were. I'm concerned about your health. You're not sleeping. You're not eating. You're not fucking that lovely woman that you seem so obsessed about."

"Do you want me to hit you again?" I hissed as I glared at him. The bruise was just now starting to fade, and I had no problems giving him another one. "I already told you that Julie is not an obsession."

"Maybe if you say it with more conviction, I'll believe you," he grinned. "Did you know that she's staying in the Sunny Side Up Motel? Why haven't you asked her to live here? She is part of your staff."

"I can't sleep with her if she lives here," I pointed out.

"Yes, but she could get murdered there or catch some disease. You're telling me that your libido is more important than her well-being? Besides, we both know that her living here won't stop you. It'll just make you feel like you're in a relationship. That's not a bad thing."

"I don't do relationships," I said pointedly. "And neither does she. In that, I think we can both agree that we're compatible."

Miles snorted. "I've known you for more than three decades, and this is the first time that I've ever thought that you were a fool."

I paused mid-sip and stared at him. "Excuse me?"

"If all you wanted was her body, you'd be over her by now. You're not, and that should tell you something."

He wasn't wrong. It told me that I needed to stay as far away from Julie Dennings as possible.

As if on cue, her sneakers squeaked across the floor as she made her way to the kitchen. I had no idea what she was doing with the money that I was paying her, but it clearly wasn't to buy new shoes. "Coffee," she moaned as she entered the kitchen. "Oh, thank God."

"Not God, although some women have said that I'm like a god," Miles teased. "In bed, of course."

Julie jumped in shock and grabbed her chest as she stared at us. "Oh. Hello. I didn't know you guys were in here."

"We're getting a late start to the morning," I muttered as I stood. "Here. Let me."

She smiled beautifully as I reached for the coffee pot, and my heart lurched. "Late night?" she asked in a quiet voice.

"I had a date," Miles announced. "Graham is an insomniac. I wonder what could be keeping him up these past few nights."

"Ignore him," I advised her as I poured the coffee. "He's an idiot. I have a favor to ask you."

Her eyes glazed over with pleasure as she took the first sip, and I watched in fascination. She was so pleased by the little things in life. Had I become so jaded that I couldn't even enjoy a cup of coffee anymore? When she swallowed, she moaned a little. "You can have anything you want," she said dreamily.

Anything? I raised an eyebrow, and she must have realized how seductive her words sounded. She ducked behind the cup. "I know that you don't work on Saturdays, but I have a fundraiser that I need to attend. I RSVPed plus one, but my date has fallen through. Would you attend with me?"

I waited for Miles to make a sarcastic remark, but he remained strangely silent. Holding my breath, I waited to see how Julie would react. I'd already told myself that if she said no, I wouldn't push the issue.

"I need to speak with Crystal to see if she'll watch him," she said slowly. "But if that's not a problem, I'd love to attend."

Relief swept through me. "He's welcome to stay here."

"No." She shook her head. "No offense, but this place has a lot to offer a kid, and I don't want him getting too comfortable here. I'm not sure how much longer we'll be."

"What do you mean?" My heart slammed against my chest. "Are you quitting?"

"Oh, it's nothing that's going to happen right around the corner. Tyler turns five at the end of the month, and I need to start doing research on schools. I want to be in a good district during the fall so he can attend some place that's suited to his needs. I think he's going to do really well in the right setting."

"I'd be happy to pay for private school." The words were out of my mouth before I could stop and think, and I felt the invisible wall slam between us. Her eyes cooled considerable.

"I appreciate the offer, but I can pay for my own son's education."

I'd hit a sensitive spot, and I needed to tread lightly. "Of course. Let me know if I can be of any assistance. I did grow up here, and I'll be happy to arrange some private interviews with the school staff if that helps you put your mind at ease. When you finish your coffee, will you meet me in my office? I have a few things that I'd like to go over."

She seemed visibly relieved when I didn't push the issue. "I'll go ahead and text Crystal in case you need to find another date."

I looked pointedly at Miles, but he just gave me a lazy

grin. "Go ahead, cousin. I'll keep Julie company while she finishes her cup of coffee. I have to admit that I'm a little turned on just watching her drink it. If she moans anymore, you could probably film it and turn it into a porno."

"Idiot," I hissed through my teeth. "I apologize for him. If he didn't look like me, I'd swear he was adopted."

Julie just laughed. "I don't mind him at all. He makes me laugh."

And I don't. Feeling a little left out, I nodded my head and climbed the stairs. I knew that I didn't need to worry about Miles seducing Julie, but at the same time, I couldn't help but feel jealous. She barely knew Miles, and she was already comfortable around him. I'd enter the room, and she'd want to run.

When she knocked on my door twenty minutes later, I was on edge. I had no idea how to act around her, and I didn't like feeling so frustrated. "Come in," I growled.

"Is this a bad time?" she asked quietly as she opened the door.

I stood. "Close it and lock it."

She obeyed without questioning why. For a moment, I thought she might flee, but there was a strange glint in her eyes as she walked to the desk. "I spoke to Crystal. She has no problems watching Tyler for the night. Is it okay if I wear the same dress from last week?"

"I'll get you a new dress."

"Would you deduct it from my paycheck? I can't keep letting you buy me dresses," she laughed.

I didn't bother telling her that the dress I had in mind for her would cost her a whole month's pay. I walked around the desk and leaned against it. "You like Miles." It wasn't a question.

"I do," she admitted. "He's charming and funny. It's hard not to like him."

"Is that all?"

Cocking her head, she studied me. "He cares for you a good deal. I like that as well. If you're asking me if I'm attracted to him, the answer is no. When I look at him, I see you. He has your eyes, although they don't carry as much weight as yours do. His hair is the same color, but I don't want to run my hands through it." She walked towards me and put a hand on my chest. "You have the same build, but I don't think of him pressed up against me."

"Christ, Julie."

"That's what you wanted to know, right? You think that I want you, but you're not sure. There's a part of you that maybe wonders if I want someone like Miles instead. After all, you two are night and day. He's easy to be with, and you're complicated. He makes me laugh and you make me spitting angry."

I reached down and lightly cuffed her wrists. "So why aren't you touching him?"

"I don't want him, Graham. I want you."

That was all I needed to hear. I lowered my lips to hers and reveled in her breathy moan as she parted her lips. I'd spent too much time away from her, and I was ravenous. In one swift move, I'd lifted her, and she wrapped her legs around me as I carried her to the desk. All the while, I never once broke the kiss.

I was rock hard and desperate to be inside her, but first I needed to taste her. Lowering her to the surface of the desk, ignoring everything that spilled off it, I slid a hand up her shorts and caressed the mound beneath her panties.

God help me, she was soaking wet.

"Graham," she gasped and lifted her hips. "Please."

"Please what?" I whispered. "Tell me what you want?"

"Everything. I want you to do everything." Her voice was breathless, and I could hear the unspoken words between us.

While we still have time.

The very thought of her leaving me ripped a primal growl from my chest as I attacked the buttons of her shorts. She lifted her hips, and I ripped them down her legs, dragging her pink panties with them. The moment they hit the floor, I'd parted her legs and slid my tongue over her.

As Julie fell back hard against the desk, I licked her until her whimpers turned to guttural moans. She was so sweet, so responsive. I wanted to spend all afternoon right here, bringing her to orgasm over and over again.

"Graham," she pleaded. "Oh God, I'm going to come. Please." Her hips bucked against me, but I anchored her down and stroked her with my tongue through her shudders and screams. Only then did I stand and unbutton my pants.

"You're mine," I hissed as I spanned her hips with my hands. "Do you understand that? Mine."

Pulling her to the edge of the desk, I entered her in one thrust. She was as tight and hot as I remembered.

She felt like home.

There was no finesse. I surged into her like a wild animal. With no regards for the future, I marked her with my teeth. I didn't give a damn who saw it. Hell, maybe I wanted people to see it. I wanted people to know that she belonged to me, and I wasn't about to let her go.

I barely held on until her muscles clamped around me as another orgasm took over, and it wasn't until I found my own release and slumped over that I realized I was naked inside her.

12

JULIE

The dark maroon fabric shimmered over my body as it clasped behind my neck and flowed down my breasts, dipping low at my back, and cupping my hips before falling to my ankles. It cinched at my cleavage with a jeweled pin, and while I tried to tell myself that it was a rhinestone, I knew it was a diamond.

I'd never worn anything like it, and as I stared at myself in the mirror, I couldn't help but feel like crying. There was a battle raging inside me. I wanted to enjoy these few fleeting moments with Graham, pretend that I could be his princess, but I also knew that it would be over soon, and while I might be in love with Graham Porter, he would never be in love with me.

Pressing my hand to my abdomen, I knew that chances were slim that he'd gotten me pregnant. There was a wild panic in his eyes even though his voice was calm as he explained that he'd forgotten the condom and came inside me. He asked me to keep him appraised of the situation. Logical. Cool. I knew that inside, he was terrified. Getting his personal assistant knocked up was not on his to-do list. Lucky for him, the timing just wasn't right.

I'd borrowed a little make-up from Crystal. A little shimmer for my lips and some eyeliner and mascara so I didn't stand out too much in what would be a crowd of glamorous women. Unfortunately, she had the most beautiful dark complexion, so I couldn't use her foundation.

I'd even borrowed her curling iron and attempted some soft curls around my face. Of course now I sported a burn mark on my arm and the curls were limp, but at least I had tried.

Pathetic.

Everyone at the party would take one look at me and know that I was a fraud, but what could I do? I wasn't about to give up a chance to spend another night in Graham's arms.

He'd wanted me to get ready at his house, but I wanted that moment when he'd knock on my door. Now, as I stared at the buzzing light outside my window and the stains on the wall, I realized how ridiculous I was being. My neighbors would take one look at my dress and steal the thing right off me.

Graham no doubt knew that, but he indulged me. When I saw his car pull up in the parking lot, I smiled. He'd been different this week. Quiet and controlled but also a little softer. Part of me wondered if it was because he thought I might be pregnant, and another part hoped that maybe I'd just misjudged him. Maybe the cold exterior didn't run as deep as I originally feared.

He'd barely knocked before I flung the door open. "I know I'm supposed to make you wait, but I don't want anyone to try and steal your car," I said hastily as I stepped outside and locked the door behind me. "I didn't really think this whole thing through."

I tried to hurry past him, but he grabbed my elbow. "Let me look at you." His voice was soft as he stepped back and stared at me. "You really are beautiful, Julie."

"Anyone would look beautiful in this dress," I muttered. "And I put on a little bit of makeup."

"I noticed. Now all I can think about is kissing you until your lips stop looking so delectable." His fingers brushed over my burn mark, and he frowned. "What happened here?" Kissing it gently, he pulled me a little closer until he could claim my lips. It was a full minute before I could break free and explain about the curling iron.

He held out his arm, and I almost giggled as I accepted it. The whole thing was laughable. The billionaire bachelor was picking me up at the hooker motel.

"What's the fundraiser for?"

"I believe it's to raise money for the children's cancer ward at the hospital."

Confused, I stared at him. "You don't know?"

"I receive a hundred invitations a week to charity events," he admitted. "I gave Darleen free reign to filter them down to ten for me to peruse. It wasn't until recently that I realized she was only sending me to fancy galas."

"I haven't seen any charity invitations."

"That's because I have them brought directly to me. I didn't know you well enough to trust that you'd put some thought into it, and I was upset by Darleen's methods. I wanted to make sure that I was more hands-on in some of the other events."

He opened the door for me, and I thought I heard a strange clicking noise. Frowning, I turned my head and looked around, but I didn't see a single soul in the parking lot with us. Sliding into the car, I waited for him join me. "What do you mean by hands-on?"

"I like working with my hands," he said with a shrug. "Whether it's building houses or volunteering at the wildlife center."

It was hard to imagine buttoned-up Graham in his silk ties hammering wood together or shoveling manure. My silence must have spoken volumes for he laughed harshly. "You think I'm the kind of man who enjoys sitting behind a desk bossing people around."

"Not at all," I said quietly. "I guess I just didn't think you understood that it's okay to shed the Porter lifestyle every now and again."

He was quiet, but it was a comfortable silence. When we arrived at the gala, all the butterflies returned to my stomach as I watched the women in beautiful dresses enter the hotel.

"Hey," he said softly as he reached over and took my hand. "I won't have you intimidated by anyone here, do you understand? There are going to be women in there who are like Darleen, and they're going to be jealous."

"Because I'm gracing the arm of Graham Porter instead of them?" I asked wryly.

"Because you are a genuine and beautiful woman." He reached over and kissed me gently, and my heart skipped a beat.

Why couldn't he have been someone just a little more attainable for me?

The valet opened the door and helped me out. I wasn't alone long before Graham walked around and took my arm, but before we could enter the hotel, people swarmed us and flashbulbs went off in our faces.

"Are you Julie Dennings?" they shouted at me. "Is it true that Tyler Dennings is the son of Jonathan Bright?"

Shocked, I froze. It was like something out of a nightmare. For a moment, Graham's arm loosened around me, and I pulled away. The questions continued as the press blocked my path into the building.

"Is it true that you were once engaged?"

"Are you living out of the Sunny Side Up Motel?"

"Are you working for Graham Porter or sleeping with him?"

"Does your son know who his father is?"

"Enough," Graham snapped as he grabbed my arm and pulled me roughly back to the valet station. "Take her home," he growled as gave them his address. The next thing I knew, they were pulling me into a service limousine. The door slammed shut behind, and I watched through the window as Graham pushed his way through the reporters and into the hotel.

Terrified that they'd find Crystal, I knocked on the window. "Excuse me. He gave you the wrong address. I need to go to the Sunny Side Up Motel. I need to get to my son."

The driver looked at me in disbelief, and for a moment, I thought he was going to ignore me. Fumbling with the buttons on the door, I finally got the glass lowered. "Please. I can't let them get to my son. If you're not going to take me, then you need to let me out, and I'll call a taxi."

"I'll take you," he said quietly. "But I don't think Mr. Porter will be very happy."

"It doesn't matter," I said tightly. "I don't think Mr. Porter is going to care one way or another where I end up as long as I don't end up back in his life."

I couldn't think of Graham's reaction to my dirty secret right now. The only thing more terrifying than the press discovering my secret was Jonathan discovering it, and I knew that if they put my picture in the newspaper, he wouldn't be far behind.

When we turned into the parking lot, my heart sank. There was already a limo waiting, and I knew that Jonathan hadn't followed the press.

They'd followed him.

Quickly, I reached for my phone. "I need you to do me a favor."

13

JULIE

Time had been good to Jonathan. The charming young man that I'd fallen love with had turned into a handsome man. He flashed a brilliant white smile to the driver as I got out of the car, and his dimples only deepened. He knew that I was spoiling for a fight, and he hadn't wanted to create a scene. Instead, he smoothed his golden locks with one hand and reached for me with the other. "Julie. Thank God," he whispered. "I've been looking everywhere for you."

"Relax," I muttered. "He's just a valet driver at the Gala I was supposed to attend. He doesn't work for Graham."

The limo pulled away, and his smile vanished. "Graham Porter," he said with an ugly twist of his mouth. "Was I not rich enough for you?"

"Look at where you're standing, Jonathan. Does it really look like I'm living in the lap of luxury?"

He must have remembered that we were out in the open. As he looked around, he grabbed my elbow and led me to the stairs. "Where is my son?" he hissed.

"You don't have a son." I angrily pulled my elbow away from him. "You made that very clear when he was born, or don't you remember? I believe your exact words were *if you tell anyone that he's mine, I'll send him overseas to boarding school, and you'll never see him again.* Does that ring a bell?"

Taking out my key, I opened the door and stepped into the motel. Once he was inside, I slammed the door shut and closed the curtains. Praying that Crystal had gotten my message and was ready, I pulled Jonathan away from the window. He stepped away and started searching the small space. "Where is he, Julie?"

Through the thin material covering the windows, I blew out my breath in relief when I saw Crystal and Tyler slip into the limousine. "You don't even know his name, do you?"

"Tyler," he snarled. "We'll be changing his last name when we're married."

"Have you lost your damn mind? You had a chance to marry me, and you chose your political career over us. Why the hell would I marry you?"

A cold smile spread across his face. "Look around you, Julie. You're living in a roach-infested motel with whores and drug dealers as your neighbors. I probably wouldn't even have to pay off a judge to get custody of him. I'll try to paint you in an optimistic light when I tell the press that you took off with my son when I caught you with a heroin needle in your arm, and I'd been searching for you ever since. Of course, it'll look much better if we have a fairy tale ending complete with the wedding of a century. They'll be talking about our painful courtship and happy ending for years to come."

He reached for me, and I didn't even hesitate before slapping him. His cheek turned red, and for a moment, I thought he might hit me back. "You think I haven't been waiting for this moment?" I asked in a calm voice as I tried to ignore the rising panic. "As soon as I found out that I was pregnant, I took precautions against you. I got a copy of the tape from the restaurant. It doesn't have audio files, but it does show you laughing at me as I handed that ring back over. I recorded the phone call from the lawyers when they told me that they didn't believe that Tyler was your son, and I recorded the phone conversation where you threatened to take him away from me."

Blood drained from his face, and I took a step closer to him. "If you thought that you were going to come here and take what you wanted from me, you've got another thing coming. I'm not the same naive girl who fell in love with you. You can try to take Tyler from me. You'll probably even succeed, but I have enough to bury your political career. No one in their right mind would back you in anything when they discover what you did to me. Now get the hell out."

"We're not done," he threatened. "The press already know."

"I don't give a damn what you tell the press. Tell them that I was fucking four guys when I was with you and that Tyler isn't yours. Tell them I'm just some whore trying to get payback. I don't care, Jonathan. All I care about is that you don't come near me or my son."

There was nothing that I wasn't prepared to do to save Tyler, and Jonathan must have known that. He left the motel without another word, and I waited an agonizing hour, texting Crystal the whole time, before I finally changed and went to my car. I'd hoped that Jonathan and the press wouldn't still be around to follow me, but even if they did, I knew they wouldn't make it past the imposing gates around the Porter mansion.

Graham's car was in the driveway. My heart leaped into my throat, but I tried to tell myself that he wouldn't throw us to the wolves. He wasn't that heartless.

Crystal, Graham, and Miles were all waiting for me in the living room when I burst in. "Tyler?" I asked wildly.

Crystal immediately came over and hugged me. "He's sleeping," she murmured in my ear as she stroked my hair. "He has no idea what's going on, and he fell back asleep in the car. Graham put him to bed. Are you okay?"

"I'm fine," I lied as I pulled away.

"Did he hurt you?" There was an edge of violence in Graham's question.

"No."

He nodded. "Crystal, you're welcome to spend the night. Miles will show you to your room."

Miles and Crystal both left the room, and I faced Graham alone. He stood and stalked towards me like a predator on the verge of an attack, but I could see the struggle inside of him. "I made some inquiries at the gala," he said hoarsely.

"And?"

"Tyler's father is the next mayor of Hartford. If he's elected, he'll probably be the next governor of Connecticut," he said in a controlled voice. "You failed to mention that part."

"He hasn't been elected yet," I pointed out.

"You made it sound like he was some dead-beat dad."

"You of all people should know that money doesn't keep someone from being a dead-beat dad. In fact, the story should sound pretty familiar to you. Rich guy decides to rebel and dates well below his station. He sweeps a girl off her feet and proposes. She thinks it's true love and happily ever after. The only difference is that while you were ready to turn your back on your family's money, Jonathan couldn't rip the ring off my finger fast enough."

He winced at the parallel. "He never wanted Tyler?"

"He told me that he'd take my son away if I even stayed in the same state, but all that changed when Mayor Jackson wanted young and old-money blood on his ballot for Vice Mayor. Jonathan realized what a black stain like a bastard child could do to his sterling reputation. He sent someone to track me down and propose again, only this time, I wasn't so naive. I would rather work three jobs to make ends meet than force Tyler into that life, and I told him as much. That night, I started running, and I never looked back."

I could see the realization dawning on him. "You pay everything in cash."

"We moved frequently, but I guess the hospital record is what did us in." I swallowed hard, still remembering the fear when Jonathan got out of the limo.

"No," Graham said harshly. "Darleen is what did you in. The press got an anonymous tip, and I'd bet every dollar in my bank account that it was her trying to drive you out of town. What does he want?"

I shrugged. "What do all men want?" I mocked. "To marry me."

"He can't force you," Graham said evenly. "You have a choice."

"I know. Unfortunately, with money comes power, and rich people have a way of getting nasty when they don't get what they want."

"He's threatening you?"

I didn't want to talk about Jonathan to Graham. All I wanted was for Graham to hold me and tell me that everything was going to be okay, but I could tell that even he was fighting to keep the white knight routine going. "This isn't your fight," I murmured. "I'm sorry that it's on your doorstep, and I'm sure that it's going to do a number on the sterling Porter reputation, but if you would just let Tyler and I spend the night, we'll be out of your hair in the morning."

"He'll follow you," Graham growled. "You won't be safe."

I couldn't help but smile when I thought of Jonathan's face when I'd threatened him. "I think he's starting to realize that I'm not going to go quietly. He might stick around for another day or two, but then he'll go home to Daddy with his tail tucked between his legs. He'll come back with big guns, but by then, I'll already be gone."

"You'll stay here until he leaves," he said roughly. "At least think of Tyler."

"Thank you."

He didn't invite me into his bed before he walked away. I consoled myself with the thought that even if he'd offered, I wouldn't have taken him up on it. Tonight, I needed to hold Tyler.

Despite what Crystal had said, my son was wide-awake when I walked into his room. "Is it true?" he asked me quietly. "Is my father here to take me away?"

"Who told you that?" I asked with a forced smile as I climbed into bed with him. Pulling him into my lap, I held him tightly and kissed the top of his head. He had little peach fuzz growing around the scar on his head.

"I heard Crystal in the car talking to the driver, and then I pretended to sleep so I could hear more. I don't want to leave you."

"Oh, baby." My heart broke. "I'm not going to let you go, okay? No matter what it takes."

"Is he a bad man?"

It took me a moment to find the right words to say to him. I didn't want him growing up thinking that his father was a monster. "Your father and I were very young when we started dating. I think a part of him loved being with me even if he didn't love me. He comes from a wealthy family, and they didn't approve of me."

"Graham is wealthy, and he approves of you," Tyler said in a small voice.

"Graham doesn't have to answer to his parents," I said wryly. Of course, that didn't mean that Graham wasn't still answering to his parents' ideals. "Anyway, your father isn't just wealthy. He's also a politician."

Tyler's eyes rounded. "Is he a president?"

"He's the vice-mayor of a big city in Connecticut. It's like a vice-president for a city. Not everyone would understand why he abandoned us, and he needs the voters to like him, so he's hoping that I'll marry him, and we'll be a family."

"I'd like to have a father," Tyler confessed to me in a small voice. "Is he my only choice?"

A lump welled up in my throat, but I forced it down. I couldn't fall apart now. "I'm not going to marry him, baby. He's never going to love you the way that you deserve to be loved. If I promise that I will love you enough for two people, will you be okay with that?"

He immediately turned in my arms and hugged my neck. "Of course, Momma. But I want you to be happy too."

No four-year-old should have to worry about his mother's happiness. In protecting Tyler from the world, I'd somehow managed to give him a whole new set of things to worry about. "As long as I have you, I'll be happy, baby," I assured him.

He didn't say anything and gently scooted on the bed

until we were side-by-side. Soon I could hear his breathing even out, but I couldn't sleep. I was too busy listening for the sound of footprints, terrified that Jonathan was going to follow through on his promise and take Tyler away from me.

14

GRAHAM

Two days had passed, and when my sources told me that Jonathan Bright still hadn't left the city, my patience fled. I was too hurt by the fact that Julie had lied to me to want to face her, and I couldn't stand the look on Tyler's face whenever I was nearby. The kid watched me as though he was waiting for me to fix everything. My photo had already graced the cover of the tabloids as the next man to have fallen into Julie's trap, and my inbox was full of people who couldn't wait to set me straight about Julie's devious ways. Every single one of them was wanting to comfort me in my time of need.

If I ever saw Darleen again, I might kill her.

Miles walked into the office with a dark scowl. "Every time I try to leave, the press follows me thinking that I'm you. How is a guy supposed to get laid with a bunch of cameras around everywhere? I've slept alone for the past two nights!"

"Poor you," I grumbled without looking up.

"I may have to make do with the kid's babysitter. What's

her name? Crystal? Sounds like a stripper, but she's pretty hot."

That made me snap my head up, and Miles grinned. "I figured that'd get your attention. What is it with you? Anyone near and dear to Julie is suddenly under your protection as well?"

"You so much as smile in her direction, and I'll do more than punch you," I said sourly. "She's trapped here as well, and I won't have you seducing her."

Miles sat in the chair and stretched his legs. "The simplest solution would be to kick Julie and the kid out. The press will follow, and since the magazines have painted her as the bad guy, no one will blame you."

"Are you trying to be an asshole?"

"Not at all. If you kick her out, then I'll finally be able to swoop in and save the day," he said with a chuckle. It faded under my withering stare, and he shrugged. "All I'm saying is that it's time to do something. Unless you like having Julie living under your roof, of course that would mean that you'd actually have to go out and face her at some point."

He wasn't wrong. I couldn't keep ignoring Julie, and the more time Jonathan had to himself, the more ammo he could gather. He didn't have to go home to his father to receive his father's protection. I'd looked into the family. The Brights had three living generations of politicians and powerful friendships that spanned half a decade. There was no stone they'd leave unturned to make sure that Jonathan went home with that kid in his arms.

Tyler was a good kid. I couldn't let that happen.

Setting my jaw, I stood. "Call the driver. I want the limo for the day," I ordered as I undid my tie. If there was one thing that Jonathan did understand, it was money. Lucky for me, I had that in spades. When I met Jonathan Bright, I wanted him to see nothing but power and influence.

"About damn time," Miles muttered as he pulled out his phone.

Half an hour later, dressed in my most expensive suit and diamond cuff links, I knocked on the door of Jonathan's suite. The man himself opened the door and scowled. "How the hell did you get past security? I specifically told them that no one was to come up to this floor."

I studied him carefully. In looks, he and I were completely different. He was the day with charming blue eyes and golden hair. I was the night with dark features and green eyes. "I assume by now that you know who I am. Powerful figures from all over the country stay at this hotel when they come to visit me. If I'd asked for your room key, they wouldn't hesitate to give it over."

His eyes narrowed. "You're bluffing."

"If you need a demonstration, I'd be more than happy to comply," I said quietly. "But if I go downstairs and ask for your room key, I'm going to return with the press and give them an open invitation."

"You think that just because you have more money than me, you can do whatever the hell you want?"

I didn't bother to wait for him to invite me in as I strode past him. I'd been in this room not three weeks ago sharing a bottle of expensive Scotch with the governor of California. "I think that's exactly what you're doing to Julie. She's under my protection."

"Damn," he chuckled. "She must have improved in the past five years because she wasn't all that good in bed when I was last between her legs. I guess she's had a lot more experience."

"If you're goading me into hitting you so you can press

charges and use it against me, you're out of luck. I wasn't just raised in the game, Mr. Bright. I'm on a whole other playing field. I suggest you leave while you still have some of your dignity intact."

His eyes widened just a little, and I could smell the fear on him. "I can only imagine the lies that she spouted to get you to defend her life like this. I broke things off with her when I realized she was sleeping with three of my friends. I guess she was strengthening her odds that one of us would knock her up and marry her."

He was hitting all the right chords, and doubt crept into me, but I wasn't walking away from here until I knew that he was leaving and never coming back. Then I could figure out what the hell I was going to do with her. "You're able to threaten her because you think she's alone and scared. I'm here to tell you that it's finished. You've lost. I have contacts in Connecticut that you will never see coming. If you even whisper Tyler's name into a judge's ear, I will marry Julie myself and adopt Tyler as my own. Not even an army could take him away then, do you understand?"

"God, she's got you wrapped around her little finger," he sneered. "I guess now she'll get to choose between two rich men. Did it ever occur to you that I realized that I made a mistake? That I want my son back because I want to get to know him?"

"No," I said coldly. "It didn't because I know all the tricks in the book. You've probably already figured out a way to pawn the kid on someone else so you never have to look at him until it comes time for your inauguration."

"Maybe. But I think that you're bluffing. I did my research on you. You're a confirmed bachelor. There isn't a chance in hell that you'd marry someone like Julie. When I met her, she was slinging drinks at a bar and flirting with anything that moved."

My back stiffened. "My feelings for Julie are something that you could never even comprehend, and I'll do whatever it takes to protect that child. Go ahead and file for custody. I'll bury you in lawyers and appeals that it won't even reach court until that boy is eighteen."

I'd won, and he knew it. When I walked out of the hotel, I knew that Jonathan Bright would never threaten Julie again. It was a bittersweet victory. I left knowing that if it had come down to it, I would have folded.

Jonathan was right. I was a confirmed bachelor. I was never going to marry, let alone marry someone who wore her heart on her sleeve. I just couldn't handle it, and now that I'd faced her demons, I had to face my own.

Her ex came here to hurt her, but I was going to be the one who broke her heart.

15

JULIE

*A*s the lawyers loomed over our shoulders, I tapped the pen in discomfort against the table. That morning I had taken a chance and signed the paperwork for an apartment. Now I was signing away Tyler's bloodline.

"And here," the lawyer said as he pointed to another line. Jonathan stood at the window with his back to me as I scrawled my name across the blank space. "Okay. You're all finished, Ms. Dennings. If you break any of the terms in this contract, Jonathan will be able to go after you with the full weight of the court behind him. I'll go make a copy for your files."

He left, and I stared at my ex. Jonathan hadn't said much during the entire meeting. "Not that I'm complaining, but why are you backing down so easily?"

"Like you don't know," he muttered as he turned to face me.

"I don't." Three days and not a word had passed before Jonathan called me that morning and asked me to meet him at his hotel room. I was unsure at first, but I knew that nothing would be able to take Tyler from the Porter Mansion, so what was the harm in meeting him?

It turned out that he needed me to sign an agreement. I would go to the press and tell them that Tyler was not Jonathan's son, and I would never publicly recant that claim. I was also giving up the right to monetary support and the use of his last name. In return, he would never attempt to take Tyler away from me.

"I guess this time you really did choose the wealthier man," Jonathan said bitterly.

"Graham? What does he have to do with this?"

For a moment, he searched my face. "You really don't know," he muttered. "Graham came to me yesterday and told me that if I tried to file for custody of Tyler, he'd marry you and adopt our boy himself. I wouldn't be able to touch him."

Graham said what? For the past three days, I thought that Graham was waiting for it to all be over so he could kick Tyler and me out, but here he was, helping us.

Telling Jonathan that he'd marry me.

"You love him," Jonathan observed coldly.

I immediately tried to change my expression. My feelings for Graham were none of Jonathan's business. "Does your father know that you're making this deal with me?"

He rubbed a hand over his face. "No. Believe it or not, I think all he wants is to meet his grandson."

"Even if it came from me?" I snorted.

Jonathan hesitated. "I'm not cut out to be a father. Or a husband. I guess you already know that, although I'll have to eventually marry and have kids. I need that family image."

God have mercy on that poor woman and his children.

He continued. "I don't want to meet Tyler. I guess I just wanted to know what kind of kid he is."

I was surprised. It hadn't occurred to me that Jonathan might actually be curious about Tyler. "He's quiet and contemplative. Smart as a whip and way too mature for someone his own age. He's a good kid."

"The pregnancy?"

"Fairly easy considering that he was my first. I should have known then that Tyler would never complain about anything. I saw a doctor at the free clinic, and I pawned the jewels that you gave me to pay as much of hospital bill as I could."

He looked at me with tired eyes. "Don't tell me any more. I guess I really didn't want to know. For what it's worth, I am sorry, Julie. There was a time when I thought that I was in love with you."

The lawyer returned with my copy of the contract, but there was nothing that I could say to Jonathan that would ease his pain. I couldn't tell him that it was all right. I couldn't even tell him that I forgave him. All I could do was stand and shake my head. "Goodbye, Jonathan," I said softly.

I drove straight to the mansion. I wanted to pick Tyler up and take him out for ice cream. I wanted to tell him that Jonathan wasn't going to take him away, and I wanted to tell him about the apartment. We couldn't move in until the weekend, but what were a few more days at the motel?

I also needed to see Graham. I needed to know if I still had a job. I needed to know if his offer to marry me had come from a place of love.

Tyler and Crystal were swimming in the pool. I found Graham holed up in his office. Even though I knew it was off-limits, I knocked on the door. "It's me," I said softly.

For a moment, I thought he wasn't going to answer. "Come in."

Opening the door, I stepped inside. After not seeing him for three days, he looked good. I knew that I looked a wreck, but you would never know that there was any type of upheaval in his life. His shirt was neatly pressed, and he looked calm. "I'm sorry that I haven't been down to check on you. Things have been busy."

I didn't bother pointing out that we were in the same house. All he had to do was walk downstairs or even hit the button on his beloved tablet on the wall. "That's all right. I wanted to thank you for letting us stay here. We'll be leaving this afternoon."

A frown crossed his face. "Jonathan has left?"

"Not yet, but I'm sure he won't be sticking around for too much longer. I just wasn't sure if you still wanted to employ me after all of this. I'd understand if I've brought too much drama down on your head."

He looked around the room uncomfortably, and my heart dropped. Of course he wasn't going to keep me on after all of this. What daydream had I been living in? "It's okay. You don't have to explain yourself."

"You're excellent at your job, and I'd be happy to give you a glowing reference. It's just that after everything that has happened, I know there will be speculation if you continue to work for me. Plus, I can't have you working here and living here too."

Living here? My heart pounded in my chest as I stared at him. Maybe I was wrong about him. After all, he did tell Jonathan that he'd marry me. "You want us to live here?" I whispered. "Graham, you have no idea what that means to me. I can't accept your offer, of course, but this is a huge step for us. I think that maybe we need to take things slow."

"Take things slow?"

"Don't worry. I do love you, but I know that this is new territory for you."

My admission wasn't just met with silence. Graham's face went slack, and I realized that I'd made a grave error. "You weren't asking me to move in because you love me," I said slowly. "I don't understand."

"Julie, listen to me," he said calmly. "With everything that happened with Jonathan, I just thought you'd feel safer here. I'm getting used to having a kid around, and I'm definitely used to having you in my bed."

In his bed? I blanched. He just wanted to keep me around for sex. Horrified, I slowly backed up. "I can't," I said hoarsely. I felt like the walls were closing in around me as I stumbled from the office into the hall.

He called my name, but he didn't go after me. Instead, I hurried to Tyler's room and blindly gathered his things. He and Crystal were already out of the pool when I reached them. "Time to go," I said with a false brightness in my voice. "I've got some great news to tell you!"

"Jonathan is gone?" Crystal breathed.

"It's over," I said as I gathered Tyler up in my arms.

It was over.

———

"What the hell are you doing?" At the sound of Graham's voice, I turned. The luggage was splayed out on the bed at the motel, and my shirt was half-folded in my hands. "I'm packing?"

"I can see that." There was an angry storm in his eyes as he stalked forward. "Tell me that you're not fucking leaving."

"Language," I hissed. "Tyler is next door with Crystal, and these walls are thin."

"You're running back to him?" His face was contorted in anger. "Why? All because he wants to put a shimmery diamond on his finger? I told you that you and Tyler could move into the mansion with me, and you're running off with him?"

"What the hell are you talking about?"

"Language," he mocked. "I thought that you were different, but you're just another gold-digging whore. Let me see if I've got this straight. You latched on to me because I've got more wealth, but when it became apparent that I wasn't ever going to marry you, you go back to the next best thing."

Stunned, I just stared at him. Pain sliced through my chest, and it hurt to breathe. "I told you that I loved you, and you told me that I could be your fuck buddy. And now you want to charge in here and judge me?"

He folded his arms over his chest. "I'm just calling it like I see it, sweetheart."

"Momma?"

I reigned in my temper and looked past Graham to see Tyler and Crystal standing in the door. My son's eyes lit up when he saw Graham.

"Hi, baby," I said as I forced a smile. "I thought I told you that I'd come get you when I was finished."

Tyler held out a book. "I know, but Crystal gave me this as a going-away present, and I didn't want you to forget to pack it."

Crystal's gaze darted between Graham and I. "Julie, is everything okay?"

"Everything is fine." I walked past him to take the book. "I'll make sure to pack this, baby, okay? Can you go back with Crystal for just a little while longer?"

"Sure. Is Graham going to visit us at our new place?" He turned to Graham and grinned. "Momma got us a perm place in the city."

"A permanent place," Crystal said softly.

"A permanent place," Tyler repeated slowly. "An apartment. Did I say it right?"

"You did great, baby," I said as Graham stared at me. "Now go on, or you'll be sleeping here again tonight."

His eyes widened in horror, and he grabbed Crystal's hand and dragged her from the room as he said a hasty goodbye to Graham.

"Julie," he whispered.

"Go away, Graham," I said tiredly. "I really don't think there's anything left for us to say. You feel bad, and you want to apologize, but it doesn't matter. You've always expected me to just want you for your money, and I don't think you're ever going to let go of that idea. You have no idea what it's like to love someone or be loved, and I won't let you hurt Tyler. We both agreed that it would be nothing more than sex, and I took it too far. That's on me. Now if you'll please leave, I need to finish packing."

"Where's Jonathan?"

I threw another shirt in the luggage. At this point, I didn't even care about folding it. "Tyler's father went home with his tail tucked between his legs. Your little threat to marry me worked. He signed away his parental rights, and I signed a piece of paper saying that I'd never tell anyone the truth."

"So you know?" His voice was dull, and I couldn't even turn to face him.

"Yes, I do. Although, I thought you were volunteering to marry me because you had feelings for me. I guess it was just a measuring contest." I threw another shirt in and slammed the top shut. I zipped it shut and waited, but there was only silence.

Graham left without another word, and it was the last crack that my shell could take. With no one there to witness it, I sank to my knees and burst into tears.

16

GRAHAM

My phone kept lighting up with messages and alerts. I'd turned it on silent, but it continued to vibrate on the counter. Annoyed, I turned it over so I couldn't see it light up anymore and lifted my empty glass to the bartender. He raised an eyebrow but didn't say anything as he poured me another drink.

"You might as well wave a sign to the press saying *I'm drunk! Take your pictures now!*" Miles grumbled next to me as he lifted a beer to his lips. "If all you wanted to do was get hammered, we could have done that in the privacy of our own home."

"My home," I snarled. "You live in New York. Why are you even here?"

He sighed. "I am trying to protect the family name. God knows that someone has to."

"Go the hell." I lifted the shot glass to my lips and closed my eyes. As I knocked it back, I barely even felt the stinging liquid slide down my throat. My entire body numb. I just wanted to feel something.

Miles scrunched up his nose. "This might be a classy joint, but I'd bet good money that woman over there is a hooker."

I glanced over my shoulder. A beautiful woman in Marilyn Monroe curls and bright red lipstick gripped the thigh of a man twice her age. "You're probably right."

"If you're here to pick up women, I'd start with her. At least she won't turn you down."

I wasn't here to pick up women. I was here because I couldn't find any alcohol in the house. I'd sent Daniel to get me more, but he hadn't returned. I had a feeling that everyone was punishing me for running Julie away.

Her face haunted me. *I love you.*

She'd told me that she loved me, and I'd called her a gold-digging whore and accused her of running back to her ex. The only way I could sink any lower is if I'd asked her to still sleep with me.

But wait, I'd already done that as well.

Miles continued as if I were paying attention. "Of course, with all the women blowing up your phone, you could probably plan an orgy. Is Darleen among those numbers."

No, she was not. In fact, I hadn't heard a peep from her. She probably realized that she'd crossed the line, that she put a child in danger, and had hidden away to the far ends of the earth. I'd thought about finding her and taking out my aggression on her, but she hadn't driven Julie away.

I did that all on my own.

"If you're feeling lonely, you're welcome to them," I muttered as I slid the phone his way.

Miles wrinkled his nose. "I do not want your leftovers."

"Most of them can only dream that they're my leftovers," I muttered. The phone buzzed again, and I dropped the phone in a glass of water. Satisfied that it wouldn't annoy me anymore, I pushed the glass away.

"You could have just turned it off."

"How can I make you leave?"

"Leave?" a breathy voice asked to my left as a beautiful woman straddled the stool. "You're not leaving, are you? I just got up the nerve to come talk to you. It would be rude if you left me now."

Her voice alone should have stirred my cock, and if that didn't do it, her huge breasts that were spilling out of her red dress should have at least given me a few dirty ideas. Instead, I just remembered the last woman I'd seen in a red dress.

Very little make-up. Small, perfect breasts. Effortlessly beautiful and completely terrified when she'd been surrounded by the press.

I needed to stop thinking about Julie. If I wasn't going to marry her, then I couldn't be pissed that she was gone. She wasn't the kind of woman you tied to the bed and left there to suit your needs. She was the kind of woman that needed to be loved around the clock.

Although tying her to my bed did give me a few ideas.

The woman next to me slid a finger seductively down my arm. "What do you say? Stick around and buy a lonely girl a drink?"

"Not interested," I said as I stood and reached for my wallet. "But I'm sure my cousin can show you a good time." I threw some bills on the bar and hurried out. The idea of being with the woman disgusted me, and that was horrifying.

I was not the kind of man to run from a beautiful woman.

"Christ's sake, we don't have the driver with us," Miles said in disgust as he followed me out. "I drove, remember?"

"Good." I slid into the passenger seat and waited.

"It has been a week, Graham. You need to pull yourself together," Miles snapped as he started the car. "Why are you doing this to yourself?"

"What else am I supposed to do?"

"You're supposed to admit that you love her and go after her," he growled in frustration. "Men like us don't get chances like this. We have to settle for women who say they love us but would probably stab us in our sleep to get our money. Julie is one of those rare women who is beautiful inside and out, and for some unknown reason, she loves you. I know you love her. I see it in your face every time you stare at that stupid boat in your office. Why do you even have that thing?"

I did love Julie. I knew it the moment that I realized just how badly I'd fucked things up. "What's the point in admitting it?" I hissed. "She's gone."

"So go after her. Put some effort into it, man. You deserve nothing less than to have her shut you down, but at least you'll know that you tried. You owe her that much. She doesn't even know how you feel. She thinks you just want her for sex."

The pain on her face kept me up at night. I'd known exactly what I'd done to her. Was Miles right? Could I make it up to her?

"I don't even know where to begin."

"Go big or go home," Miles said with a smile. "Buy her a real boat. Set off some fireworks. Hell, buy her an island. I hear women love that."

"No," I said as I settled into the seat and closed my eyes.

A sense of peace and calm settled over me. "She wouldn't want flash or money."

"So what does she want?"

She'd already told me what she wanted, but I was too busy trying to keep her at arm's length to listen to her.

All she wanted was me.

17

JULIE

"Hi, Momma."

Startled at the sound of Tyler's voice, I whipped my head around. My back ached from wiping down the booths, but I couldn't move to my son's side fast enough.

"Tyler! What are you doing here? You're supposed to be at home!" Had something happened to Crystal? She was supposed to be watching Tyler for me. I reached for my apron thinking that I must have missed a phone call from her.

"It's okay. Daddy brought me."

My blood ran cold. "No," I whispered. After all of this, Jonathan wasn't going to break his promise to me. He couldn't. "Baby, what have I told you? You don't go anywhere with Jonathan. He's dangerous."

Tyler scrunched up his nose. "Fathers are biological, but Daddies come from the heart."

Relief swept through me, but I still had no idea what Tyler was talking about. "Baby, what do you mean? Who brought you here?"

"He said that Daddies love us no matter what, and he's hoping that you will still love him even though he was a block-head and said things that you didn't deserve to hear." Tyler spoke carefully as though he'd rehearsed every word. He reached into his pocket and pulled out a velvet box. "He promises that even if you say no, he'll still love us no matter what."

I stared at the ring box. It was almost too much to hope that if I looked up, he'd be standing out there, waiting for me. Terrified that I'd be disappointed, I reached for the box and flipped it open.

I could tell that it was an antique. The huge diamond and seven surrounding emeralds glittered in the sunlight. Apparently, Tyler's job wasn't over yet. "He said that if you think it's ugly as sin, he'd get you something else, but he wanted you to know that you were worthy of his family ring and that even if you said no, he knew that he'd never find anyone else to give it to."

Lifting my eyes, I glanced out the window. Sure enough, Graham stood against the car, his entire body tense as he watched me.

Still in so much control. "Baby, can you wait here for me?" I asked softly.

"What are you going to say, Momma?"

"I don't know yet, but I guess I should figure it out."

Tyler nodded in agreement, and I gripped the ring as I walked outside. His eyes watched me warily. "You're not going to throw it at me, are you?"

"Using my son is a pretty low blow," I retorted as I stopped right in front of him. "You have a lot of nerve."

"No one has ever told me that I lacked nerve." A slow grin spread across his face. "At least, not until you claimed that I had no idea what it was like to love. You couldn't be more wrong, Julie. I know exactly what it's like to be in love. I just didn't have the nerve to say it out loud until now."

I folded my arms. "You still haven't said it out loud."

"I love you, Julie Dennings. I love you, and I love that ridiculously mature son of yours. In the past two weeks, I've been driving myself crazy. I missed ruffling his hair, and I missed waking up with you in my arms. I drove you away because I thought you were a weakness, but you're not. You're my strength. I have never felt so alive, and it terrified me. I said the most horrible things to you, and I'm sorry. I've never regretted anything more. I deserve nothing more than for you to tell me to go to hell, but I couldn't let you go until you knew the truth. I want you to be Juliette Porter. I want to adopt your son. I want to help raise him, and maybe a whole mess of other kids with you. I love you, Julie."

"Christ." I hadn't expected him to say all that. I figured he'd just grunt out that he loved me and expect me to fall into his arms.

Of course, I would have, too. That's how much I loved Graham Porter.

"I know you hate that I'm rich, but I swear that I won't be my father. Although Daniel loves that kid, he won't be raising him. We will. That kid will be able to do anything that he wants to do, and I won't force him to be something that he's not. I don't give a damn about the reputation of the Porter name. I just want him to be happy. I want you to be happy."

"You can stop now," I whispered. The blood drained from his face, and I took out the ring and slipped it on my finger. "It is a bit big, but maybe if we remove the emeralds, I can live with it."

"Oh God." Relief swept over his face, and he reached for me. "I thought you were going to say no."

"Graham, I was going to say yes the minute you told me that you loved me, but you just kept right on talking." I laughed as he picked me up and whirled me around in the parking lot before kissing me smack on the lips.

Turning my head, I could see Tyler beaming in the window. "I guess you were my prince after all," I murmured.

"You're no damsel in distress," he laughed. "You're a Queen. You always have been. I think you're the one saving me."

————

We married a month later, and the press went wild. Everyone wanted to know more about the mysterious woman who'd finally won over Graham Porter, and he'd just told everyone the truth.

I was his personal assistant and his savior.

————

THE END

DID YOU LIKE *Keeping Secrets from the Billionaire?*

Then you'll LOVE Bound by the Billionaire.

I wanted her the moment I saw her.

I never thought she would get caught up in one of my games.

I've never been with someone who was both soft and willing and yet somehow so hard to get.

But my world is changed now.

If only I knew how to change hers for the better.

———

I have responsibilities to take care of. I have a son.

I can't keep letting him take me like this.

In the storage room at work. (True, he owns the building, and many more like it.)

But I'm not ready to fall in love again no matter how he makes me feel, especially not someone as unstable and eccentric as him.

If only my body would let me forget the first time I tasted him and felt those hands.

The way he bound me as part of one of his bored rich boy games.

Start reading Bound by the Billionaire now.

BOUND BY THE BILLIONAIRE (PREVIEW)

A BAD BOY, SINGLE-MOM, BILLIONAIRE ROMANCE

1

———

Kim Davidson tried to pull together some energy. Her shift at Elixir had been crazy busy. From the minute she'd arrived, she was running. Her boss's mother-in-law was turning seventy and the party of twenty was demanding and, worse still, bad tippers. That would mean less money this week, and already her mother was complaining when she'd left in the morning.

"You know Derek really needs some new shoes. His feet are cramped in these," she said while getting Kim's son ready for school.

"I know, Ma, I'm trying. I start the new cleaning job at the gallery tonight that'll help. Things will be better. Promise."

Her mother kissed her on the cheek. "Kimmy, honey, I know you try so hard. Your ex-husband should be paying for some of this, you know. Useless man!"

"Please, Ma, I don't want Bruce involved in my life, or in Derek's life. We'll be fine." She bent down to her son. "Won't we, D?"

"Yes, Mama," the little boy said.

Kim kissed him. "You be a good boy at school. I'll try to get home before you fall asleep."

Her mother didn't understand. Yes, she'd like money from her ex-husband—that would make everything easier—but the price she'd have to pay would be too much. He wouldn't just give them money and leave them alone; she knew him too well. If he gave them money, he'd expect to be involved in their life, and she would not have that. Never again. She was fine without a man, better than she'd ever been. She was in control of things. This was all just a tiny blip; she'd soon be back on track. Just a bad patch to get through. Once she got going with this regular job cleaning at the gallery and then with the two waitressing jobs, she ought to be able to save some money and get them all sorted out. It'd been tough for her mother too ever since her father died—one of the reasons Kim lived with her. But Kim was going to get them all out of trouble. They'd be fine; they just needed to give her a bit of time. There was no need to get her ex involved in things. Kim was done with men anyway. She'd learned her lesson; life never was a fairy tale. No prince on a white horse was going to save her. She would need to do it for herself.

She arrived at the front of Rive Gauche Gallery and tried to forget the five hours of running around waiting on demanding old women and men with grabby hands. A new job needed new energy. She took a deep breath and opened the door. She entered the glass-fronted building and found a security guard at the reception desk.

"Are you here for the opening?" he asked.

"Opening?"

"The opening of the Clara Dancy exhibit?"

"No, I'm part of the cleaning crew. My first night."

"Oh?" The middle-aged man's voice went up as if

somehow his prospects had just improved. "So you'll be working nights? With me?"

Kim looked him over. Obviously Italian. Obviously middle-aged. And obviously married. *What was it with men? Why did they think every woman was interested in being hit on?*

She ignored his question. "Where's Sonya Lando?"

Sonya was Kim's friend from high school. While Kim had gone off to her disastrous marriage with Bruce, Sonya got straight to work. Though she only had a high school diploma, she'd done well for herself. She was already a manager at Rive Gauche and had helped Kim get this new cleaning job.

"She's at the party in gallery one, down that hall." The security guard pointed to the left, and Kim set off in that direction.

"I didn't get your name," he called after her.

"Because I didn't give it to you," Kim said, walking away.

Kim knew which room it was because she heard the music and talking from quite some distance. At the entrance, she saw that she was underdressed in her jeans and blouse, so was reluctant to get inside of the room. Most of the men were in suits and many of the women in long evening gowns. Kim's gaze was drawn to the paintings on the walls, big bold colors in purples, dark blues, splashes of red. And everywhere on the wall, figures of women, their beautiful bodies draped across beds, entangled in the arms of their lovers, gently holding their children. The paintings were so gorgeous Kim was swept away and didn't notice when Sonya came up to her.

"I remember in high school you were a beautiful painter," Sonya said.

"It feels like a million years ago." Kim smiled at her

friend, who looked sophisticated in a long black sheath with a massive silver necklace and strappy silver sandals to match.

The memory of how she used to love painting made Kim sad. She was suddenly being reminded of her life before Bruce. Her life when it had so many possibilities, when she was going to be a painter— the time when every day brought a new dream. The time before he crushed her aspirations with his constant talk: telling her she was nothing, telling her she could never do anything with her life. And now here she was, a single mother waiting tables and working as a janitor. Maybe he had been right about her. In any case, those dreams of becoming a famous painter seemed destined to never be fulfilled.

She shook her head, attempting to shake those horrible memories back to where she kept them locked-up. She'd learned how to ignore the things that brought her down. Those were Bruce's words anyway, not hers, just words with no meaning. She knew one day she'd be back on track and all of her still-to-be-discovered dreams would come true; they had to, not only for her, but for her son Derek too.

"I'm here and ready to work," Kim said. "That's some security guard you got there, already trying to make his moves on me."

"Who? Frank?" Sonya laughed. "Ignore him. It's just his way; he's a nice enough guy."

"So where do I start?" Kim asked.

"Wow, you're an eager beaver! Chill. You can't do much until the opening is over anyway. Do you want to vacuum around these people?" She laughed at her own joke. Kim smiled. What she really wanted was to finish as quickly as possible, get home, kiss her likely already sleeping son, and climb into her own bed. She didn't say that to Sonya though.

"Let's go and get some champagne," Sonya said, taking Kim's arm to lead her inside.

Kim stopped. "I don't know. Maybe I can wait out with Frank until the party's over."

"Don't be silly! Why do you want to pass up free champagne? That's not the Kim Davidson I used to know."

Kim knew she wasn't the Kim Sonya used to know. But that was not the problem. "I don't think I'm dressed appropriately."

Sonya looked her up and down. "Artists don't care about such things. You should see what the woman who painted these paintings is wearing. I think it's her smock she wears in her studio."

Kim still hesitated. Sonya pushed her around the corner. She took her necklace off and put it around Kim's neck, pulling the collar of her white blouse up for effect. She took a bright red lipstick from her silver handbag and quickly swiped it across Kim's full lips, then dabbed it with a tissue from her bag. Then she pulled the hair tie out of Kim's long blonde hair and fluffed it up it so it fell around her shoulders in long golden waves.

"Jesus!" Sonya said, standing back and looking at Kim. "You're more beautiful than you were in high school, and in high school I was so jealous of you I could have bit your nose off if I got the chance."

They both laughed at that. Kim caught a reflection of herself in the shiny plating on the corner of the wall, and she was shocked. *Was that her?* She worked all of the time, and when she wasn't working she was trying to spend time with Derek or sleeping. Taking care of herself had fallen off the radar. There was just no time for that anymore. Who was that woman? Kim thought when she looked at herself. *Where had she gone?*

"I'm simply dying of thirst! I might collapse right here if I don't get some champagne. Can we go into the party now? Please!" Sonya begged Kim.

Kim laughed. "Always the drama queen, hey, Sonya? Okay, let's go!"

2

————————

Robert looked out at the calm surface of Lake Michigan and wished he was somewhere else—anywhere else. Anyone looking at the scene would have thought he was crazy. A beautiful summer day, out on his own yacht, beautiful women at his beck and call, champagne, waiters to serve them—how could anything be wrong? It was everyone's dream. Robert wondered what was wrong with him. He had everything, but he felt so empty, as if he had nothing.

He had arrived at twenty-six, a billionaire with companies and properties all over the world. His legacy was well-established; he had nothing to prove anymore. Why was that not enough? Why did he feel so restless and unfulfilled? Why did this life he lived seem so pointless?

A tall brunette in a bikini, with new breasts and a pouty mouth advertising that it was not all natural, passed by and took his hand. "Come on deck and dance with us, Robert."

"Later," he said. He smiled at her, and she disappeared. Robert spotted Debra, his PA, near the door and waved her over. She was always where he was and absolutely loyal. She took care of everything for him, just as she'd always done.

"Sir?" Debra said. She was old-school respectful, something Robert used to like, but even that annoyed him lately.

"Call me Robert, Debra," he said.

"Yes, sir."

Robert gave up. "I'm sneaking downstairs to my bedroom. Tell people looking for me I'm sick. I want to be alone for a while."

"Yes, sir... I mean, Robert." At least she was trying. It would take time.

Robert lay on his bed in the spacious bedroom fitted out with oak wardrobes and dressing tables attached to the walls for the rough seas his yacht sometimes encountered. He'd traveled in it to Greece and South Africa, even to Australia a few times. It was his home when he was not in Chicago in his lakefront penthouse on the twenty-fifth floor of one of the buildings he owned in the city. The ground floor was his gallery, Rive Gauche, one of the more prestigious in the country. Art was one of Robert's passions, and finding and promoting new artists he loved was one of the few things in his life that still gave him real joy. He kept to the background though. He didn't like being seen as the owner or the benefactor. Few people knew what he actually did, and he liked it that way.

He looked up to the ceiling, sighing. He was sick in a way. He had been for some time. What was wrong with him? Was he lonely? Could it be as simple as that? Lonely with people constantly around him.

Of course he missed his parents, but the accident had been over three years ago now. Surely he was over the initial shock of the loss. It was a tragedy when their private plane crashed in the Andes, but Robert sometimes thought it was better they died together. Theirs had been a love story like no other, one Robert could only dream of ever having, and he doubted either one of them would have survived happily on their own. Robert was an only child, so he often felt lost without them, but the way he felt lately was more than that. His life seemed so meaningless. Nothing really challenged him anymore. Everything was easy and unexciting. Living the playboy life had lost its fun.

He rolled to his side. Soon the yacht would dock and the crowd would leave and he would be free of them, at least for a while. He had the opening of the Dancy show at the gallery tonight. He loved her paintings and would like to purchase one or two tonight for his house in Paris, but he didn't look forward to seeing the same vacuous people that always attended such functions in Chicago. They were always there more for being seen than for appreciating the art. They would, as usual, be fawning over him in the insincere manner he'd come to loathe.

But then he reminded himself of his plan, and a surge of excitement passed through his body. He'd thought of it some weeks before, and it had not left his mind since. He'd read a story about an employee at the Louvre who stole the Mona Lisa—Vincenzo Peruggia. Something about that stuck with him. He imagined himself stealing a painting; just the thought made his blood race with excitement, something he never felt nowadays. To plan and execute such a thing successfully began to fill his mind and, oddly, it gave him a reason for living, something beyond his normal life.

Tonight he planned to implement what he'd laid out for himself. Tonight he intended to commit a perfect crime: to steal a painting from his own gallery and not get caught. He smiled thinking about it as he slowly drifted off to sleep.

"Sir? Sir?"

Robert opened his eyes, confused. Where was he?

"Sir, sorry to disturb you, but we've been docked for three hours now, and I fear if you don't get up soon you will miss this evening's engagement." Debra stood to the side, as if embarrassed, holding his tuxedo in one hand.

Robert sat up on his bed and looked out the window. He was still on the yacht. It was dark, the city lights sparkling in the distance. He felt refreshed though; the long sleep had been exactly what he needed. He checked the clock and saw it was already 8:30. He'd be late for the opening—he'd better get going. He had a big night ahead of him.

Robert couldn't keep his mind still. All he could think of was his plan. Once the party was over and the crowd cleared out, when all was quiet, he would sneak back in and do it. Which painting would he steal? He decided since this was really just a practice run to see if he could get away with it, he would steal the painting that he'd purchased shortly after he'd arrived. It was small and in a good position in the gallery. And it would harm no one. The painter would have been paid, and he would not claim from his insurance for the loss. It was the perfect choice for his first attempt.

He milled around the crowd, trying to pay attention to the conversations about new business acquisitions or charities that were being started, gossip about who was sleeping with whom. He had interest in none of it.

Mrs. Vallier stood far too close to him and ran her hands up and down Robert's well-defined biceps, felt clearly through his jacket while she talked. "You know we only just returned from Cannes. It was amazing. We missed you this year, Robert."

She smiled at him, a smile meant to remind him of their rendezvous in a cheap hotel up the coast. Mrs. Vallier, though married and a few years old than Robert, was an energetic lover if little else.

"Perhaps next year," Robert said, moving off.

He stood before the painting he'd purchased, the one chosen for the night's escapade. It was a small painting, little bigger than two of his hands wide. The naked woman, for all of the paintings were of gorgeous naked women in all of their beauty, lay across a rumpled bed. A red blanket was pushed to the side, and one of her arms was thrown above her head, her long blonde hair spread around her like a halo, her other hand cupping between her legs, a slight smile on her face. He loved everything about the painting. The woman looked satiated after lovemaking of the long and luxurious kind. He would enjoy holding the painting in his hands; he got excited just imagining it. Art should move a person, and this painting moved him.

He turned looking away from the painting, and there she was.

Across the room, a woman, with the same spectacular blonde hair as the woman in the painting. She was dressed casually, as if clothes were nothing to her, that her real substance was herself— who she was— not the accoutrements that money could buy. So unlike the other women that filled up the room. It was such a new and refreshing manner, Robert could not look away from her. She wore a white blouse with a bold silver necklace and little makeup except for a slash of bright red lipstick on her perfect, natural lips. She looked directly at him. She noticed he was staring at her, but she did not look away. Nor did she move toward him, as most of the women in the room would have done, the hunt begun. She stayed where she was.

The gallery was packed with people. Robert pushed through them to get nearer to this extraordinary woman. He was finally next to her, though she was facing away from him. The crowd pushed him into her, his body against her back, and he bent his face slightly toward her golden hair and thought how it smelled of sunshine and summer and fields of green grass. His body, against his will, was filling with adrenaline, the excitement moving through him just being near her. He could not remember ever being so affected by a woman. He felt lost in her somehow.

She turned to him, and she was more beautiful up close than she was from across the room.

"Hello," she said. "I thought I saw you looking at me from over there in the corner. Did you want something?"

"No," he said. "Only to meet you, I guess." He held out his hand. "Hi, I'm Robert."

She smiled at him and her face lit up, and his breath caught in his throat. Had he ever met such a beautiful woman before? So beautiful and yet she seemed completely unconcerned about it and the effect she was having on him.

"Hi, Robert. I'm Kim. Kim Davidson."

To Keep Reading Bound By The Billionaire Find it here.